Edward Robert Bulwer Lytton

Poems of Owen Meridith

The Earl of Lytton

Edward Robert Bulwer Lytton

Poems of Owen Meridith
The Earl of Lytton

ISBN/EAN: 9783337407018

Printed in Europe, USA, Canada, Australia, Japan

Cover: Foto ©Andreas Hilbeck / pixelio.de

More available books at **www.hansebooks.com**

The Canterbury Poets.

Edited by William Sharp.

POEMS OF OWEN MEREDITH (THE
EARL OF LYTTON).

*_** FOR FULL LIST OF THE VOLUMES IN THIS SERIES, SEE CATALOGUE AT END OF BOOK.

POEMS OF OWEN MEREDITH (THE EARL OF LYTTON). SELECTED, WITH AN INTRODUCTION, BY M. BETHAM-EDWARDS.

AUTHORISED EDITION.

"Und so do ist der Dichter zugleich Lehrer, Wahrsager, Freund der Götter und der Menschen."—WILHELM MEISTER.

LONDON :

WALTER SCOTT, LIMITED,

24 WARWICK LANE.

NEW YORK: 3 EAST FOURTEENTH STREET.

CONTENTS.

—◆—

INTRODUCTION.

As the nosegay indicates the luxuriance of the garden, so should a selection epitomise the genius of the poet. Old acquaintances are reminded of many a familiar flower, strangers are enticed to enter. If the first may miss more than one especial favourite, they will still feel grateful for so much beauty presented to them in small compass; if the last cannot roam over the entire domain, they are compensated by the gift of lily or rose. "The poet," writes the all-sympathetic Goethe, "is alike teacher, seer, the friend of gods and men." A more modest yet gracious and self-rewarding function is that of the poet's interpreter, of one who culls choicest blossoms of poesy for others, pointing to the pleasance wherein they grow.

It is no easy task to review in a few short pages the poetic career of Owen Meredith and the Earl of Lytton, one and the same person, yet characterised by work so widely divergent in scope and treatment as to suggest two individualities. No less might doubtless be averred of many another poet, but authorship and personality in their case being united from the onset, such contrasts are less striking. With a constancy, almost universally witnessed, a constancy often illogical enough, the vast majority of readers prefer the poet's earlier to his later utterances—Owen Meredith to the Earl of Lytton. Such is the verdict passed on most writers winning the laurel crown in early youth. Perhaps the world is too lazy, too pre-occupied, to bestow the same amount of thought and sympathy upon their maturer achievements; it is so difficult, moreover, to believe that the same wand can enchant us twice over! But may there not in this case be another reason? When a writer has pleased, his readers, for the most part, wish to go on being pleased in the same way; no matter how often he repeats himself, if the repetition is up to his standard, nothing more is expected or asked of him. When every new work is a wholly new departure, the striking out of a new path, then he is sure, at least for a time, to forfeit popularity; he is under the necessity of creating his public. Thus it has come about that the poetic achievements of Lord Lytton's maturer years still await the fame they deserve. In the words of an able critic, "The first work in which Lord Lytton's genius did itself full justice was *Glenaveril*, published in 1885. By this time Owen Meredith, the poet, had well-nigh been forgotten in the Earl of Lytton, diplomatist and statesman. The great originality of this work, its wealth of ideas and creation of character, obtained no adequate recognition."* My endeavour has been to make the accompanying selection a representative one, revealing the various aspects of a many-sided genius, the subtle and the sportive, the picturesque and the reflective, the dramatic and psychological. It has also been my plan to avoid fragmentariness, and give, with one or two exceptions, only such pieces as are complete in themselves. This arrangement has necessarily led to the exclusion of descriptive passages of great brilliance and beauty, but which, gems removed from their setting, were more suited to a volume of mere extracts.

Middle-aged lovers of poetry well remember the pleasure with which they hailed the appearance of *Clytemnestra.* Seldom indeed has a first attempt secured its youthful author such poetic rank. This noble dramatic poem, like the "Iphigenie auf Tauris" of Goethe, is no mere echo of the old Greek drama, but an interpretation in the modern spirit of one of its most striking episodes. In the "Agamemnon," writes Dr. Donaldson, the queen's jealousy of Cassandra and guilty connection with the worthless Ægisthus, who does not make his appearance till towards the end, are scarcely touched upon as motives, and remain in the background.† In Owen Meredith's *Clytemnestra,* her vacillating lover, like Macbeth, eager to reap the fruits of crime, but shrinking from the crime itself, is a prominent figure, the protagonist of the play, the

* See the *Scots' Review*, 1887.
† Donaldson's *Theatre of the Greeks.*

faithless wife adducing reprisals for her slaughtered child in order to excuse the murder of her husband.

> " Whate'er I am, be sure that I am that
> Which thou hast made me,—nothing of myself,"

is her passionate outpouring to Ægisthus, calling forth the fervid reply—

> " Oh, you are a Queen,
> That should have none but gods to rule over I
> Make me immortal with one costly kiss !"

Readers will do well to turn from the extract here given, a piece of description complete in itself, to the account of the same event in the old drama.

The difference between the ancient and modern spirit is strikingly brought out. In Æschylus the sacrifice at Aulis reads like a page out of the "Prometheus Bound." All is rugged, stern, awe-inspiring. The poet of our own day softens the picture, a magic spell overtakes us as we read, the harmony of the numbers takes from the horror of the scene described.

Touching too, and serving as a relief to the sombre story, is the scene between the young Orestes and his sister Electra, the affectionate, neglected daughter of the murderess Queen, who, wedded to a herdsman, is the heroine of one of Euripides' charming plays.

With *Clytemnestra* appeared "The Earl's Return," abounding in weird description, and

also some shorter pieces, several of which, old
favourites, are here reproduced.

Owen Meredith's next volume, *The Wanderer*,
was received even more warmly than the first,
and here the task of selection has been
comparatively easy. "The Portrait," "The
Marquise," "Midges," "A Love - Letter," are
among the poet's brilliant triumphs of this period.
"To a Woman," in later volumes called "The
Last Wish," is an entire love-story and life-story
in four lines.

A few years later appeared *Lucile*. The author,
in his touching dedication to his illustrious father,
spoke of the doubt and discouragement with which
he gave his new poem to the world, following a
path in which he could discover no footprints
before him either to guide or warn.

In reality *Lucile*, although an experiment, pos-
sessed all the elements of popularity. This novel
in verse appealed alike to young and old, to the
practical and romantic. It contained deep human
interest, a note of lofty moral aspiration, abundant
knowledge of the world, a moving story having a
picturesque background; lastly, the narrative was
in flowing, graceful verse. The local colour of
the early portion, that part of the scene laid in the
Pyrenees, is especially attractive; as we read, we
breathe the pine-scented air of the forest, gaze
upon the deep gorges and flower-besprinkled
dells, hear the thunder of the storm amid the
mountains. *Lucile* is said to be the most popular
narrative poem in America, but has not yet been

given to the English public in a form within reach of all. A cheap edition of this charming story would be a public boon.

In the following year (1861) the *Songs of Servia* were given to the world. "What they are," wrote the poet in his Introduction, "let the reader decide. What they are meant to be is nothing more than a rude medium through which to convey to other minds something of the impression made upon my own by the poetry of a people among whom literature is yet unborn; who in the nineteenth century retain, with the traditions, many also of the habits and customs of a barbarous age; and whose social life represents the struggle of centuries to maintain under the code of Mahomet, the creed of Christ.

"It is indeed this strange intermixture of Mahometan with Christian associations which gives to the poetry of the Servs its most striking characteristics. It is the sword of a Crusader in the scabbard of a Turk. That, however, which mainly distinguishes this from all other contemporary poetry with which I am acquainted is the evidence borne on the face of it, of an origin, not in the heads of a few but in the hearts of all. This is a Poetry of which the People is the Poet!"

Awaiting a popular re-issue of the *Serbski Pesme*, all familiar with these "native wood-notes wild" will welcome old favourites here, whilst readers now introduced to them for the first time will enjoy a poetic treat. Artless, joyous, or plaintive by turns, we are reminded as we read of the national Slavonic music, especially of the songs of the Steppes, as lately rendered in Paris by a band of Russian vocalists. Just as the physiognomies of the singers were strikingly contrasted with their voices, the men having many of them wild half-Tartar faces, whilst their singing was of the sweetest, tenderest, most pathetic imaginable; so in the *Songs of Servia*, the naïveté, even ruggedness of the measures, are allied with airiest fancy and melancholy grace. In both, too, is conspicuous a certain *espièglerie*, a roguishness, in keeping with themes so primitive, an art so untutored.

From the succeeding volumes, *Chronicles and Characters* (1869), selection has necessarily been limited. The length of these poems, mostly narrative, has shut them out of a volume limited in size, yet nowhere else are the author's wealth of fancy and mastery of versification more apparent. Lord Lytton revels in rhyme, and has made some developments of it peculiarly his own, a point returned to later on. These poems are all rhymed, and abound in striking description. Take, for example, the passage entitled "A Blind Man sees far," from the "Siege of Constantinople." Alone sits the sightless old Doge Dandolo, and beholds with his mental vision the triumph of Venice in the East. He

" ——saw, as in a trance,
Constructed out of golden circumstance,
The steadfast image of a far-off thing
Glorious and full of wonder. . . .

　　　　　　Clear upspring
　Into the deep blue sky the golden spires
　That top the milk-white towers, like windless fires ;
　O'er gardened slopes, slant shafts of plumy palm
　Lean seaward from hot hillsides breathing balm.
　Green, azure, and vermilion, fret with gold.
　Blaze the domed roofs in many a globèd fold
　Of splendour, set with silver studs and discs :
　And, underneath, the solemn obelisks
　And sombre cypress stripe with blackest shade
　Sea terraces, by summer overlaid
　With such a lavish sunlight as o'erflows
　And drops between thick clusters of wild rose
　And clambering sparweed, down the sleepy walls
　To the broad base of granite pedestals
　That prop the grated ramparts, round about
　The wave-girt city ; whence flow in and out
　The wealth and wonder of the Orient World :
　And, high o'er all this populous pomp, unfurled
　In the sublime dominions of the sun,
　And fanned by floating Bosphorus breezes won,
　To waft to Venice each triumphant bark
　The winged and warrior Lion of St. Mark ? "

Or take this description of Cyprus from " Caterina Cornaro " :—

" In Cyprus, where 'live Summer never dies,
　Love's native land is.　There the seas, the skies,
　Are blue and lucid as the looks, the air
　Fervid and fragrant as the breath and hair,
　Of Beauty's Queen ; whose gracious godship dwells
　In that dear island of delicious dells,
　Mid lavish lights and languid glooms divine.
　There doth she her sly, dainty sceptre twine
　With seabank myrtle spray and roses sweet
　And full as, when the lips of lovers meet

The first strange time, their sudden kisses be
There doth she lightly reign ; there holdeth she
Her laughing court in gleam of lemon groves,
The wanton mother of unnumbered Loves ! "

Goethe says somewhere that painters should live in palaces. Doubtless Lord Lytton's poems owe much of their rich colouring to the writer's early acquaintance with some of the loveliest and most favoured regions under the sun. Owen Meredith is indebted to the diplomatist, the ambassador. Readers, compelled to do most of their travels by proxy, may here transport themselves to those romantic lands, which by turns became his home.

The *Chronicles and Characteristics* must not, however, be regarded entirely from the objective point of view. In some of these pieces reflecting various phases of life, thought, and history, the framework is made subsidiary to the idea, the background to the story. A deep, passionate note of sympathy with suffering humanity, is struck in "Misery" and "The Dauphin"; subtle psychological problems are worked out in "The Botanist's Grave," with its moral—

" The world, perchance after all, knows already enough,
     what is wanted   •
Is not to know more but how to *imagine,* the much that
     it knows."

Orval, or the Fool of Time, appeared in 1869. Suggested by an analysis of a Polish poem, the work is quite unlike any other by the author. Orval, in turn, suggests Faust, Manfred, and Cyprian of Calderon's famous play. The key-note to his story or to theirs is—

> " We are fooled
> By time and plagued with granted prayers. Henceforth,
> Let man, whose realm is the Actual, leave
> To the great God, what by the greedy grasp
> Of his impatient passion, man destroys,
> —'The Ideal Beauty!' "

The dialogue is in blank verse, and the treatment of a weird, complex story, highly imaginative and poetic.

Fables in Song belong to 1874. It is not easy to characterise these two volumes, containing poems so directly opposed to each other alike in form and spirit. Lord Lytton has made fable-land his own, maybe it is the poetic region in which he most delights. Here we find his charming testimony to Æsop and the fanciful but touching description of "The Forest whose name is Fable," hidden from the busy, unreflective crowd, but accessible to artless, childlike natures.

The stories which may be strictly classified as fable, deal not only with the sayings and doings of the animal world, but of the supposititious sayings and doings of inanimate nature. Every object, natural or artificial, is made a sentient, observant entity, and thus endowed, is able to afford alternate warning, amusement, or instruction. Many of the parables abound in humorous touches. It is a curious region to which we are transported, a region wherein men and women hold only the secondary place, or perhaps do not so much as exist, whilst even nature is sometimes kept in the background or banished altogether. A consummate knowledge of the world and of the springs moving human conduct is here displayed.

Some of the poems, on the other hand, can hardly come under the category of fable at all. To this list belong " The Wheat-Ear," and " The Thistle," each full of tenderest meaning, and showing the closest observation of nature.

A lapse of nearly ten years brings us down to the publication of Lord Lytton's epic of modern life, *Glenaveril.* Why is it that whilst *Lucile* attained immediate popularity, this far more brilliant, original, and finished work yet awaits the recognition it deserves ? The reason is not hard to discover. *Lucile*, sparkling, full of life, colour, and movement, appealed to the vast majority of readers. It is a book for relaxation, not study, one we may put in our pocket, like a novel, for spare moments.

Glenaveril belongs to a wholly different stamp. The plot is very involved. It occupies two closely-printed volumes ; it contains political satire sure to offend very large numbers ; last of all, it exacts attention.

On the other hand, the two foster-brothers, whose life-story is so intricately and tragically interwoven, the old German pedant, the modern

Robinson Crusoe, Cordelia—could not the author have invented a name for his heroine?—all these are charming creations. Interspersed with the narrative are brilliant passages, reflective and dramatic, also some of those fables and fairy tales in which Lord Lytton has hardly a rival, and his high level of artistic finish is everywhere maintained.

Yet even sympathetic readers might desire certain excisions. The work would undoubtedly gain much by judicious condensation. A poem sent into the world in the form of two bulky volumes is unavoidably handicapped from the practical point of view—to put it bluntly, as a marketable commodity. Only one or two extracts are given from *Glenaveril*, but readers must go to the poem itself for any grasp of its scope and character.

The following verses may be taken as the key-note:—

> " What she sees in love
> Is life's most sacred mission from above.
>
> A mission to which few are called perchance,
>   And fewer still are chosen, to effect
> The revelation and deliverance
>   Of a sublime evangel, whose elect
> Evangelists, each worldly circumstance
>   That contradicts its truth, must need reject . . .
>
> How should I know what passes in the high
>   Ethereal regions of which souls like hers
> Are the inhabitants! Such regions lie
>   Beyond my reach, where Earth with Heaven confers!
> Yet though I cannot comprehend them, I

The more revere those wondrous characters
Whose lives bestow on all the human race
A higher dignity, a grander grace.

And in that girl I humbly recognise
One of those rare surpassing souls whose glow
Gladdens the world with beautiful surprise,
Like great creative poets."

The speaker is a blunt, shrewd, matter-of-fact American. In George Eliot's novels, the painful problem almost invariably before us is the subjection of the more elevated nature to the inferior. In *Glenaveril* we find a cheerfuller, we will hope, truer theory. The effect of ideal characters upon those infinitely below them, only attracted upward by virtue of sympathy, is subtly and beautifully worked out.

With the little volume entitled *After Paradise; or, Legends of Exile* (1887) closes this brief survey. Concerning the poet's latest effort I cannot do better than quote from a critic before alluded to. "The best of these poems are not only superior to anything Lord Lytton has yet produced, but are such as to entitle him to a very high place among contemporary poets. The merit, however, of these last is of a peculiar order, and that, perhaps, not likely to attract a very large circle of readers. The peculiarity consists in a combination of two elements—the fantastic and the philosophical. Lord Lytton transports us into a world of airy fancy, a world purely imaginative; yet through all the imagination the reflective vein runs so strongly as to make it clear that as much importance is attached to the underlying thought as to the poetical medium in which it is conveyed. In this peculiar department of poetry Lord Lytton appears to us to have established something like a claim to pre-eminence. The 'Legend of Music' and 'Uriel' are poems as original as they are beautiful, and we do not think any other living writer could have produced them. . . . For originality, for wealth of poetic diction, for the harmonious flow of its verse, and for the subtle and creative fancy which it displays, the 'Legend of Music' deserves to take its rank with the best poems the century has produced."

The *Legends of Exile* form a series, and must be read as a whole to be understood and appreciated. On this account, also because of its length, much to my regret, I have been obliged to leave out the "Legend of Music," which would best convey the spirit and range of the volume.

Whence comes the Ideal? This is the problem the poet has set himself to work out, on lines of his own. Imbued with the philosophy of Plato, he regards,

"Our birth as but a sleep and a forgetting "—

knowledge as a reminiscence of what we have experienced in a former condition.

" Those shadowy recollections,
Which, be they what they may,
Are yet the fountain light of all our day,
Are yet a master-light of all our seeing."

The Ideal is therefore memory, a bright ray shot up from a sun that has for ever sunk behind our mortal horizon. It will easily be seen how well the Biblical story of the Fall lends itself to such a theory. Music, love, poetry, are recollections, dreams, the Ideal itself a golden vision, never to be grasped. Pessimistic as is this doctrine, and opposed to the modern Socialistic dictum, "The Golden Age is before us and not behind," we must remember that the poet's ideal refers to spiritual things only, not to the material side of existence, which certainly shows a progressive and no retrograde movement. Is there not truth here? Can we look about us and feel sure that we are any nearer an inner ideal of life than Plato? Is there not a certain measure of truth in Renan's wail over the gradual vulgarisation of life and society?*

In "Uriel" and "Strangers," detached pieces forming no part of *The Legends of Exile*, the same theme is handled with great power and pathos.

The first is a parable which each reader may interpret after his own fashion. Be they "bright-eyed desires," passions, enthusiasms, or ideals, the Legions which Uriel led forth to do battle with the world, at the bidding—shall we say of duty,

---

* "Peut-être la vulgarité générale sera-t-elle un jour la condition du bonheur des élus. La vulgarité Américaine ne brûlerait point Bruno, ne persecutérait point Galilée. Nous n'avons pas le droit d'être fort difficiles."
—Renan, *Souvenirs de Jeunesse.*

ambition, love, or imagination?—lie vanquished around him. He is but chief of a slaughtered band. Yet once more the voice makes itself heard, urges him forth a second time to become the sport of destiny, to be finally crushed and overcome. In the cold, cynical atmosphere of disenchantment he hears another voice—

"Some say it is Despair,
And others say it is Experience."

"Strangers" will appear at first sight to many readers fragmentary, obscure, perhaps incoherent. Those who read and re-read will, we think, accord it a foremost place among Lord Lytton's shorter poems. The deepest note of human feeling is here struck. And it is one of sadness, even of despair. The ideal world of spiritual-minded humanity is a disillusion. Love, able to re-create after its own image, becomes in turn victim of its magnanimity. The mission of the lofty, angelic nature, is to love, to sacrifice self and to suffer!—a conclusion sad enough, but borne out by the history of the world from the beginning until now.

Our poet, whose sympathy is ever with what is elevated and noble, leaves a more inspiriting message to the work-a-day world.

" Deep in Nature's undrained Cornucopia,
Every good that man seeks, he shall find :
And to fools, only fools is Utopia
The abode of the hopes of mankind.

For whate'er God hath made for man's good
  He hath granted man means to attain ;
Say thou therefore ' I will,' not ' I would,'
  Undeterred by the coward's disdain."

Having now surveyed the harvest, we offer this sheaf of golden grain, feeling sure that the reader's thanks, as well as our own, will be heartily accorded the generous author who has permitted such lavish gleanings.

M. B.-E.

NOTE.—In accordance with Lord Lytton's wishes, the poems, as far as possible, appear according to the date of their original publication. Many of the early pieces are from revised versions.

Poems of Owen Meredith

(The Earl of Lytton).

From "*CLYTEMNESTRA.*"

CLYTEMNESTRA.

X.—*Chorus.*

THE winds were lull'd in Aulis; and the day,
Down-sloped, was loitering to the slumbrous west.
There was no motion of the glassy bay.
The black ships lay abreast.
Not any cloud would cross the hollow skies.
The distant sea boom'd faintly.   Nothing more.
They walk'd about upon the yellow shore;
Or, lying listless, huddled groups supine,
With faces turn'd towards the flat sea-spine,
They plann'd the Phrygian battle o'er and o'er;
Till each grew sullen, and would talk no more,
But sat, dumb-dreaming.   Then would some one rise,
And look up at the high mast-heads with haggard,
⸗ hopeless eyes.
Wild eyes—and, crowding round, yet wilder eyes—
And gaping, languid lips;
And everywhere that men could see,
About the black-ribb'd ships,

Was nothing but the deep-red sea;
The deep-red shore;
The deep-red skies;
The deep-red silence, thick with thirsty sighs;
And daylight, dying slowly.   Nothing more.
The tall masts stood upright;
And not a sail above the burnish'd prores;
The languid sea, like one outwearied quite,
Shrank, dying inward into hollow shores,
And breathless harbours, under sandy bars;
But, rushing swift into the hot broad blue,
The intense, sultry stars
Burn'd strong, and singed the simmering welkin thro';
And, all below, the sick and steaming brine
The spill'd-out sunset did incarnadine.

At last one broke the silence; and a word
Was lisp'd and buzz'd about, from mouth to mouth;
Pale faces grew more pale; wild whispers stirr'd;
And men, with moody, murmuring lips, conferr'd
In ominous tones, from shaggy beards uncouth:
As though some wind had broken from the blurr'd
And blazing prison of the stagnant drouth,
And stirr'd the salt sea in the stifled south.
The long-robed priests stood round; and, in the gloom,
Under black brows, their bright and greedy eyes
Shone deathfully; there was a sound of sighs,
Thick-sobb'd from choking throats among the crowd,
That, whispering, gather'd close, with dark heads
      bow'd;
But no man lifted up his voice aloud,
For heavy hung o'er all the helpless sense of doom.

Then, after solemn prayer,
The father bade the attendants tenderly

Lift her upon the lurid altar-stone.
There was no hope in any face; each eye
Swam tearful, that her own did gaze upon.
They bound her helpless hands with mournful care;
And loop'd up her long hair.
Back from the altar-stone,
Slow-moving in his fixèd place
A little space,
The speechless father turn'd.   No word was said.
He wrapp'd his mantle close about his face,
In his dumb grief, without a moan.
The lopping axe was lifted over-head.
Then, suddenly,
There sounded a strange motion of the sea,
Booming far inland; and above the east
A ragged cloud rose slowly, and increased.

Not one line in the horoscope of Time
Is perfect.   O what falling off is this,
When some grand soul, that else had been sublime,
Falls unawares amiss,
And stoops its crested strength to sudden crime!
So gracious a thing is it, and sweet,
In life's clear centre one true man to see,
That holds strong nature in a wise control;
Throbbing out, all round, the heat
Of a large and liberal soul.
No shadow, simulating life,
But pulses warm with human nature,
In a soul of godlike stature;
Heart, and brain, all rich and rife
With noble instincts; strong to meet
Time calmly, in his purposed place.
Sound through and through, and all complete;
Exalting what is low, and base;

Enlarging what is narrow, and small;
He stamps his character on all,
And with his grand identity
Fills up Creation's eye.
He will not dream the aimless years away
In blank delay,
But makes eternity of to-day,
And reaps the full-ear'd time.   For him
Nature her affluent horn doth brim,
To strew with fruits and flowers his way—
Fruits ripe, and flowers gay.

The clear soul in his earnest eyes
Looks through and through all plaited lies;
Time shall not rob him of his youth
Nor narrow his large sympathies.
He is not true, he is a truth,
And such a truth as never dies.
Who knows his nature, feels his right,
And, toiling, toils for his delight;
Not as slaves toil: where'er he goes,
The desert blossoms with the rose.
He trusts himself in scorn of doubt,
And lets orb'd purpose widen out.
The world works with him; all men see
Some part of them fulfill'd in him;
His memory never shall grow dim;
He holds the heaven and earth in fee.
Not following that, fulfilling this,
He is immortal, for he is!

O weep! weep! weep!
Weep for the young that die;
As it were pale flowers that wither under

CLYTEMNESTRA.

The smiting sun, and fall asunder,
Before the dews on the grass are dry,
Or the tender twilight is out of the sky,
Or the lilies have fall'n asleep;
Or ships by a wanton wind cut short,
And wreck'd in sight of the placid port,
Sinking strangely, and suddenly—
Sadly, and strangely, and suddenly—
Into the black Plutonian deep.
O weep ! weep ! weep !
Weep, and bow the head,
For those whose sun is set at noon:
Whose night is dark, without a moon :
Whose aim of life is sped
Beyond pursuing woes,
And the arrow of angry foes,
To the darkness that no man knows—
The darkness among the dead.
Let us mourn, and bow the head,
And lift up the voice, and weep
For the early dead !
For the early dead we may bow the head,
And strike the breast, and weep;
But, oh, what shall be said
For the living sorrow ?
For the living sorrow our grief—
Dumb grief—draws no relief
From tears, nor yet may borrow
Solace from sound, or speech ;—
For the living sorrow
That heaps to-morrow upon to-morrow
In piled up pain, beyond Hope's reach !
It is well that we mourn for the early dead,
Strike the breast, and bow the head;
For the sorrow for these may be sung, or said,

CLYTEMNESTRA.

And the chaplets be woven for the fallen head,
And the urns to the stately tombs be led,
And love on their memory may be fed,
And song may ennoble the anguish;
But, oh, for the living sorrow—
For the living sorrow what hopes remain?
For the prison'd, pining, passionate pain
That is doom'd for ever to languish,
And to languish for ever in vain,
For the want of the words that may bestead
The hunger that out of loss is bred.
O friends, for the living sorrow—
For the living sorrow—
For the living sorrow what shall be said?

XX.—*Chorus (conclusion)*.

Only Heaven is high.
Only the Gods are great.
Above the searchless sky,
In unremovèd state ;
They, from their golden mansions,
Look over the lands, and seas;
The ocean's wide expansions,
And the earth's varieties:
Secure of their supremacy,
And sure of affluent ease.
Who shall say "I stand !" nor fall?
Destiny is over all !
Rust will crumble old renown.
Keep and castle, tower and town,
Bust and column tumble down;
Throne, and sceptre; crest, and crown.

Destiny is over all!
One by one, the pale guests fall
At lighted feast, in palace hall;
And feast is turn'd to funeral.
Who shall say " I stand !" nor fall?
Destiny is over all!

THE MAGIC LAND.

.

From " *THE WANDERER.*"

—

THE MAGIC LAND.

I.

By woodland belt, by ocean bar,
  The full south breeze our foreheads fann'd,
And lightly roll'd round moon and star
  Low music from the Magic Land.

II.

By ocean bar, by woodland belt,
  More fragrant grew the glowing night,
While, faint thro' dark blue air, we felt
  The breath of some unnamed Delight;

III.

Till Morning rose, and smote from far
  Her elfin harps. Then sea, and sky,
And woodland belt, and ocean bar,
  To one sweet note, sigh'd *Italy!*

DESIRE.

THE Night is come,—ah, not too soon!
  I have waited her wearily all day long,
While the heart, now husht, of the feverish noon
  In his burthen'd bosom was beating strong.
But the cool clear light of the quiet moon
  Hath quench'd day's fever, and forth in song,
One by one, with a buoyant flight,
Arise day's wishes releast by night.

The night is come!   On the hills above
  Her dusky hair she hath shaken free,
And her tender eyes are dim with love,
  And her balmy bosom lies bare to me.
She hath loosen'd the shade of the cedar grove,
  And shaken it over the long dark lea,
She hath kindled the glow-worm, and cradled the
    dove,
  In the silent cypress tree.

O Hesperus, bringer of all sweet things,
  Hear me in heaven, and favour my call!
Bring me, O bring me, what naught else brings
  The one sweet thing that is sweeter than all.
Bring me unto her, or bring her to me,
  Whose unseen eyes I have felt from afar.
I feel I am near her, but where is she?
I know I shall find her, but when shall it be?
  O hasten it, Hesperus star!

My heart, as a wind-thrilled lyre,
　　Throbs audibly.　Bright in the grove,
Like mine own thoughts taking fire,
　　The star-flies hover and rove.
Arise! go forth, keen-eyed, swift-wing'd Desire!
　　Thou art the Bird of Jove,
And strong to bear the thunders that destroy,
Or fetch the ravisht flute-playing Phrygian boy.
　　Go forth athwart the world, and find my love!

————

FATALITY.

I.

I HAVE seen her,—the Summer in her soft hair,
　　And the blush-rose husht in her face,
　　　And the violet hid in her eyes!
And my heart, in love with its own despair,
　　Speeded each pulse's passionate pace
　　　To that goal where pain is the prize.

II.

Hair, a Summer of glories fill'd
　　With odours!　Lips that are ever Spring;
　　　The budding and birth of all joys that be,
All blossoms that brighten, all beams that gild,
　　All birds that gladden, all breaths that bring
　　　Delight to the spirit in me.

III.

And oh, that smile of divine surprise,
　　That slid out slowly, and lapp'd me round
　　　With a rosy rapture of warmth and light !
It began in the dark of her deep blue eyes,
　　And, o'erflowing her face and her faint lips,
　　　drown'd
　　　Past, present, and future, quite,

IV.

In a sea of wonder without a shore.
　　As tho', while you gaze at a drop of dew,
　　　It should silently open, and softly rise,
And spread to a deluge, and cover you o'er.
　　So round me, and over me, greaten'd and grew
　　　The smile of those sorrowful eyes.

V.

What sort of a world will the world be now ?
　　Oh, never again what the world hath been !
　　　And how happen'd this marvellous change ?
What my old life meant I begin to know,
　　But I know not what may this new life mean.
　　　It is all so sweet and strange !

VI.

Enough to be sure of,—that, hand in hand,
　　We have seen, with each other's eyes,
　　　The heavens grow happier o'er us,
And, here below, in the lovely land,
　　As, there above, in the blissful skies,
　　　A world of beauty before us !

THOUGHTS AT SUNRISE.

THE lark leaves the earth,
 With the dew on his breast.
And my love's at the birth,
 And my life's at the best.
What bliss shall I bid the beam bring thee
 To-day, love?
What care shall I bid the breeze fling thee
 Away, love?
What song shall I bid the bird sing thee,
 O say, love?
For the beam, and the breeze,
And the birds—all of these
(Because thou hast loved me) my bidding obey, love.
 Now the lark's in the light,
 And the dew on the bough.
And my heart's at the height
 Of the day that dawns now.

————

THOUGHTS AT SUNSET.

I.

JUST at sunset I would be
In a bowery island.   Tree
Interlacing tree shall strew
Sighs and shadows over me ;
Whom some Odysseian crew
(Far too foolish, or too wise,
Here in happy bowers to be
Woo'd away from labour due

To their chieftain's stern emprise)
Putting forth in haste to sea,
Half an hour before moon-rise,
Left behind them, fancy-free,
Careless of their shouts and cries,
Mine own pleasure to pursue
Thro' the warm isle's witcheries.
And, if anywhere the breeze
Shall have stirr'd those island trees,
I, forthwith, may haply view
(Lying, lull'd by leafy sighs,
Underneath in grassy ease)
Who knows what of strange and new ?
Some white naiad's wistful eyes ?
Or a wood-nymph's rosy knees ?
Or a faun's hoof peeping thro' ?
These, or stranger things than these !

II.

Nay! already Fancy, tired
Of her isle too soon desired,
Lightly borne on laughing wind
Leaves the lazy land behind.
For the seaborn airs that sigh
All about the rosy sky
Seem, in wishful tones, to say
" Rise, O rise, and haste away!"
Seen from sea is sunset best.
Forth into the boundless west,
Ere yon sinking sun be set !
Where the seas and skies are met,
And the lights are loveliest
Round the deathbed of the day,
Find me on the breezy deck

Of some fleet felucca,—nest
Of old seabirds, born for prey,
Who these shallow seas infest.
Fancy me brown-faced as they,
With hawk eyes that watch one speck
'Twixt the crimson and the yellow;
Which shall be a little fleck
Of cloud, or gull with outstretcht neck,
To Spezia bound from Cape Circello.
With a sea-song in mine ears
Of the bronzen buccaniers,
While the night is waxing mellow,
And the helmsman slackly steers—
Leaning, talking to his fellow,
Who hath oaths for all he hears;
Each thief swarthier than Othello!

III.

Ah, but wander where she will,
Here is Fancy's birthplace still;
And, tho' far and wide she roam,
Long she may not leave her home.
Dear, I have not any want
Deeper than to be with you,
When the low beam, falling slant,
Stains the heaven with rosy hue,
And, with shuddering pleasure, pant
The awaken'd woodlands blue;
And about his leafy haunt,
While the stars are faint and few,
The tumultous firefly flashes;
And such languor softens thro'
The deep lights 'neath these long lashes
As the heart, it steals into.

First inspires, and then abashes.
Just to touch your hand—one touch,
The lightest—more would be too much ;
Just to watch you leaning o'er
That wandering window-rose . . . no more!

TO IRENE.

As, in lone faërylands, 'twixt coral shelf
And beryl shaft, to deck the moonlit cave
Where haply dwells some beautiful Queen-Elf,
Laden with light and music, a spent wave
Strews its unvalued sea-wealth (pearl and gem
Sent up in homage from the Deep, her slave !)
Then sinks back, sighing, into the salt sea ;
So, from my life's love-laden deeps, to thee
I pour these poems.   Do not thou contemn
Gifts offer'd to thee only.   Let them have
All they were born for,—not the more or less
Of aught that grudging hucksters ever gave
For such sea-treasures with a greedy guess
At this or that pearl's price in weigh'd-out pelf,
—But place in the imperial diadem
Of thine own fay-born beauty's queenliness.
More worth is in them than mere words express.
Such pearl-buds, torn from buried branch and stem
Of life's deep-hidden growths, attest love's stress.
Look down, and see in my sad silent self,
Beneath all words, where love lies fathomless ;
And so, dear love, for love's sake value them.
Love's words are weak, but not love's silences.

AN EVENING IN TUSCANY.

CLOSE, O close and clasp, the pages
  Of that too-long-pamper'd book !
Leave all poets of past ages,
  You, my living poem ! Look,
Down the summer-colour'd weather
  The sweet day begins to sink !
And the thought that we're together
  Is the sole thought I can think.
Cool the breeze mounts, like this Chianti
  Which I drain down to the sun.
So away with your green Dante !
  Turn the page—where we begun—
At the last news of Ulysses—
  A grand image, fit to close
Such great golden eves as this is,
  Full of splendour and repose !
And look down now, o'er the city
  Sleeping soft among the hills—
Our dear Florence ! That great Pitti
  With its steady shadow fills
Half the town up : its unwinking
  Cold white windows, as they glare
Down the long streets, set one thinking
  Of the old Dukes who lived there;
For one knows them, those strange men, so—
  Subtle brains, and iron thews !
There, the gardens of Lorenzo—
  The long cypress avenues—
Creep up slow the stately hillside
  Where the merry loungers are.
But far more I love this still side—
  The blue plain you see so far !
Where the shore of bright white villas

Leaves off faint: and faint the stream
Creeps from bridge to bridge as still as
   Some husht gladness thro' a dream.
On the mountain slopes in glory
   Lingers still the sinking sun :
But up here—slow, cold, and hoary,
   Climb the olives, one by one:
And the land looks fresh : the yellow
   Arbute-berries, here and there,
Growing slowly ripe and mellow
   Through a flush of rosy hair.
For the Tramontana last week
   Was about.   'Tis scarce three weeks
Since the snow lay, one white vast streak,
   Upon those old purple peaks.
So to-day among the grasses
   One may pick up tens and twelves
Of young olives, as one passes,
   Blown about, and by themselves
Blackening sullen-ripe.   The corn too
   Grows each day from green to golden.
The large-eyed windflowers forlorn too
   Blow among it, unbeholden.
Bind these bounteous curls from falling,
   O my beautiful, my own !
'Tis for you the cuckoo's calling.
   Hark ! that plaintive mellow moan
Up the hillside, floating nearer,
   Past the two white convent towers,
Where the air is cooler, clearer,
   Round our calm and pleasant bowers.
Oh, that night of purple weather !
   (Just before the moon had set),
You remember how together
   We walk'd home ?—the grass was wet—

The long grass in the Poderé—
  With the balmy dew among it:
And that nightingale—his airy
  Song—how joyously he sung it !
All the fig-trees had grown heavy
  With the young figs white and woolly:
And the fireflies, bevy on bevy
  Of soft sparkles, pouring fully
Their warm life through trance on trances
  Of thick citron-shades behind,
Rose, like swarms of loving fancies
  Through some rich and pensive mind.
So we reach'd the Logia.   Leaning
  Faint, we sat there in the shade.
Neither spake.   The night's deep meaning
  Fill'd the silence up unsaid.
Hoarsely through the cypress-alley
  A civetta* out of tune
Tried his voice by fits.   The valley
  Lay all dark below the moon.
Until into song you burst out—
  That old song I made for you
When we found our rose—the first out
  Last sweet Spring-time in the dew.
Well ! . . . if things had gone less wildly—
  Had I settled down before
There, in England—labour'd mildly—
  And been patient—and learn'd more
Of how men should live in London—
  Been less happy—or more wise—
Left no great works tried and undone—
  Never look'd in your soft eyes—
I . . . but what's the use of thinking?
  Hark ! our nightingale—he sings—
          * Screech-owl.

Now a rising note—now sinking
  Back in little broken rings
Of warm song, that spread, and eddy—
  Now he picks up heart—and draws
His great music, slow and steady,
  To a silver-centred pause !

THE STORM.

I.

BOTH hollow and hill were as dumb as death,
  While the heavens were moodily changing form.
  And the hush that is herald of creeping storm
Had made heavy the crouch'd land's breath.

II.

At the wide-flung casement she stood, full height,
  With her glittering hair tumbled over her back.
  And, against the black sky's supernatural black,
Shone her white neck, scornfully white.

III.

I could catch not a gleam of her anger'd eyes,
  (She was sullenly watching the storm-cloud roll),
  But I felt they were drawing down into her soul
The thunder that darken'd the skies.

IV.

" And so do we part, then, for ever?" I said.
  " O speak only one word, and I pardon the rest !"
  For sole answer, her white scarf over her breast
She tighten'd, not turning her head.

V.

" Ah, must sweet love cruelly play with pain ?
    Or," I groan'd, " are those blue eyes such deserts
        of blindness
    That, O woman, your heart hath no heed of un-
        kindness
To the man on whose breast it hath lain ? "

VI.

Then alive leapt the lightning.   She turn'd, in its
        glare,
    And the tempest had clothed her with terror : it
        clung
    To the folds of her vaporous garments, and hung
In the heaps of her heavy wild hair.

VII.

One word broke the silence : but one : and it fell
    With the weight of a mountain upon me.   Next
        moment
    All was bellowing thunder, and she from my com-
        ment
Was gone ere it ceased.   Who can tell

VIII.

How I got to my home in the horrible hills,
    Thro' black swimmings of storm and burst seams of
        blue rain ?
    Sick, I lean'd from the lattice, and dizzy with pain.
And listen'd—and heard the loud rills,

IX.

And look'd,—and beheld the red moon low in air.
   Then my heart leapt . . . I felt, and foreknew, it,
      before
I heard her light hand on the latch of the door !
When it open'd at last,—she was there !

X.

Childlike, and wistful, and sorrow-eyed,
   With the rain in her hair, and the tears on her cheek,
   Down she knelt—all her fair forehead fallen and meek
In the light of the moon—at my side.

XI.

And she call'd me by every caressing old name
   She of old had invented and chosen for me,
   While she crouch'd at my feet, with her cheek on my
      knee,
Like a wild thing grown suddenly tame.

XII.

'Twas no vision !　This morning, the earth, prest beneath
   Her light foot keeps the print.　'Twas no vision last
      night !
   For the lily she dropp'd, as she went, is yet white
With the dew on its delicate sheath !—

SONG.

I.

As the one star that, left by the morning,
  Is more noticed than all night's host,
As the late lone rose of October,
  For its rareness regarded the most,
As the least of the leaves in December
  That is loved as the last on the tree,
So sweetest of all to remember
  Is thy love's latest promise to me.

II.

We must love, and unlove, and, it may be,
  Live into, and out of anon,
Lovetimes no few in a lifetime,
  Ere lifetime and lovetime be one.
For to love it is hard, and 'tis harder
  Perchance to be loved again.
But if living be not loving,
  Then living is all in vain.

III.

To the tears I have shed, and regret not,
  What matters a few more tears?
Why should love, that is present for ever,
  Be afraid of the absence of years?
When the snow's at the door, and the ember
  Is dim, and I far o'er the sea,
Remember, beloved, O remember
  That my love's latest trust was in thee !

THE FIRST FAREWELL.

I.

I MAY not kiss away the tears that still
    Hang on the lids which those loved eyes enshrine.
I may not weep away the tears that fill
    These aching eyes of mine.

II.

Sleep on, sad soul, shelter'd from love and pain!
    Or haply shelter love from pain with thee
In thy sweet dreams.   When we two meet again,
    'Tis but in dreams 'twill be.

FORBEARANCE.

I.

CALL me not, love, unthankful, nor unkind,
    That I have left my heart with thee, and fled.
I were not worth that wealth which I resign'd,
    Had I not chosen poverty instead.

II.

Leaving, I love thee best.   I dare not swerve
    From my soul's rights,—a slave tho' serving thee.
I but forbear more nobly to deserve.
    The free gift only cometh of the free.

TO A WOMAN; OR, THE LAST WISH.

SINCE all that I can ever do for thee
Is to do nothing, this my prayer must be:
That thou may'st never guess nor ever see
The all-endured this nothing-done costs me.

A LOVE-LETTER.

I.

My love,—my chosen,—but not mine! I send
  My whole heart to thee in these words I write;
So let the blotted lines, my soul's sad friend,
  Lie upon thine, and there be blest, at night.

II.

This blossom bruised whose purple blood will stain
  The page now wet with the hot tears that fall—
(Indeed, indeed, I struggle to restrain
  The weight of woe that breaks thus, spite of all!)

III.

I pluck'd it from the branch you used to praise,
  The branch that hides the wall. I tend your
    flowers.
I keep the paths we paced in happier days.
  How long ago they seem, those pleasant hours!

IV.

The white laburnum's out.   Your judas-tree
　Begins to shed those crimson buds of his.
The nightingales sing—ah, too joyously !
　Who says those birds are sad ?   I think there is

V.

That in the books we read, which deeper wrings
　My heart, so they lie dusty on the shelf.
Alas ! I meant to speak of other things
　Less sad.   In vain ! they bring me to myself.

VI.

I know your patience.   And I would not cast
　New shade on days so dark as yours are grown,
By weak and wild repining for the past,
　Nor vex sad memory with a bootless moan.

VII.

For hard enough the daily cross you bear,
　Without that deeper pain reflection brings;
And all too sore the fretful household care,
　Free of the contrast of remember'd things.

VIII.

But ah ! it little profits, that we thrust
　From all that's said, what both must feel, unnamed,
Better to face it boldly, as we must,
　Than feel it in the silence, and be shamed.

A LOVE-LETTER.

IX.

Irene, I have loved you, as men love
　Light, music, odour, beauty, love itself,—
Whatever is apart from, and above,
　Those daily needs which deal with dust and pelf.

X.

And I had been content, without one thought
　Our guardian angels could have blush'd to know,
So to have lived and died, demanding nought
　Save, living dying, to have loved you so.

XI.

My youth was orphan'd, and my age will be
　Childless.　I have no sister.　None, to steal
One thought away from all you are to me,
　And yours is all I am, and think, and feel.

XII.

My wildest wish was vassal to your will:
　My haughtiest hope, a pensioner on your smile,
That did with light my barren being fill,
　As moonlight glorifies some desert isle.

XIII.

I never thought to know what I have known,—
　The ecstasy of being loved by you:
I never thought within my heart to own
　One wish so blest that you should share it too:

XIV.

Nor ever did I deem, contemplating
  The many sorrows in this place of pain,
So strange a sorrow to my life could cling,
  As, being thus loved, to be beloved in vain.

XV.

But now we know the best, the worst. We have
  Interr'd, and prematurely, and unknown,
Our youth, our hearts, our hopes, in one small grave,
  Whence we must wander, widow'd, to our own.

XVI.

And if we comfort not each other, what
  Shall comfort us in the dark days to come?
Not the light laughter of the world, and not
  The faces and the firelight of fond home.

XVII.

And so I write to you; and write, and write,
  For the mere sake of writing to you, dear.
What can I tell you that you know not? Night
  Is deepening through the rosy atmosphere

XVIII.

About the lonely casement of this room,
  Which you have left familiar with the grace
That grows where you have been. And on the
    gloom
  I almost fancy I can see your face:

XIX.

Not pale with pain, and tears restrain'd for me,
　　As when I last beheld it; but as first,
A dream of rapture and of poesy,
　　Upon my youth, like dawn on dark, it burst.

XX.

Perchance I shall not ever see again
　　That face.　I know that I shall never see
Its radiant beauty as I saw it then,
　　Save by this lonely lamp of memory,

XXI.

With childhood's starry graces lingering yet
　　I' the rosy orient of young womanhood,
And eyes like woodland violets sunny-wet,
　　And lips that left their meaning in my blood.

XXII.

I will not say to you what every day
　　Unworthy preachers preach to worthless love
' Dance the graves bare, if pipe and tabor play,
　　And call faith folly, if the world approve ! '

XXIII.

I will not cant that commonplace cf friends,
　　Which never yet hath dried one mourner's tears,
Nor say that grief's slow wisdom makes amends
　　For aching hearts and desolated years;

XXIV.

For who would barter all he hopes in life,
  To be a little wiser than his kind?
Who arm his spirit for continued strife,
  When all he cared to keep is left behind?

XXV.

But this, this only . . . Love in blackest woe,
  Still lovelier than all loveless happiness,
Hath brilliancies of joy they never know,
  Who never knew the depth of love's distress.

XXVI.

My messenger (a man by danger tried)
  Waits in the courts below; and ere our star
Upon the forehead of the dawn hath died,
  Heart of my heart! this letter will be far

XXVII.

Athwart the mountain, and the mist, to you.
  I know each robber hamlet.   I know all
This mountain people.   I have friends, both true
  And trusted, sworn to aid whate'er befall.

XXVIII.

I have a bark upon the gulf.   And I,
  If to my pain I yielded in this hour,
Might say . . . 'Sweet fellow-sufferer, let us fly!
  'I know a little isle which doth embower

XXIX.

' A home where exiled angels might forbear
  Awhile to mourn for Paradise.' . . . But no !
Never, how dark soe'er my fate, and drear,
  Shalt thou reproach me for that only woe

XXX.

Which neither love can soothe, nor pride controul;
  Which dwells where duty dies: and haunts the
    void
Of life's abandon'd purpose in the soul;
  The accusing ghost of what itself destroy'd.

XXXI.

Farewell, and yet again farewell, and yet
  Never farewell,—if farewell mean to fare
Alone and disunited. Love hath set
  Our days, in music, to the self-same air;

XXXII.

And I shall feel, wherever we may be,
  Even though in absence and an alien clime,
The shadow of the sunniness of thee,
  Hovering, in patience, through a clouded time.

XXXIII.

Farewell ! The dawn is rising, and the light
  Is making, in the east, a faint endeavour
To illuminate the mountain peaks. Good-night. .
  Thine own, and only thine, my love, for ever !

THE MESSAGE.

BECAUSE she hath the sweetest eyes,
The bluest, truest,—and more wise
Than woodland violets wild in wood
To make wholesome the earth, and good;
Because she hath such glad gold hair
That nothing in the laughing air
Of the lusty May, at morn,
When all that's bright and glad is born,
Ever was so glad and bright;
And, therewith, a hand more white
And warm than is the warmèd coat
Of whiteness round a meek dove's throat,
Yet withal so calm, so pure,
No ill passion may endure
That serenest hand's chaste touch;
And because my love is such
That I do not dare to speak,
Of the changes on her cheek,
Which the sunrise and sunset
Of her luminous thoughts beget,
Nor of her rose-sweet mouth, that is
Too sweet to kiss, or not to kiss,
'Tis aye so sweet and savorous;
And because (to comfort us
For what throbbings of sweet pain
Come, and go, and come again,
Till the wishful sense be full,
Gazing on aught so beautiful)
Such innocent wise ways she knoweth,
And so good is all she doeth,—
All she is,—so simple, fair,
Joyous, just, and debonair,

That there is none so ignorant
Of worship, nor with soul so scant
Of visitations from above,
But, seeing her, he needs must love,
And purely love, her,—and for this,
Love better everything that is;—

Therefore now, my Songs, will I
That ye into her presence hie,
Flying over land and sea,
Many an one, that sever me
From the sweet thing that hath the sleeping
Joy of my shut heart in keeping.
But, that when ye hence be gone
Into the bounteous region
Of that bright land over sea
Wherein so many sweet things be,
Where my Lady aye doth dwell,
Ye her dwelling dear may tell,
Nor its special sweetness miss
In midst of many sweetnesses;
Yet awhile, my Songs, delay
Till I have told ye, as I may,
All the fairness of the place
That is familiar with the grace
And glory of my Lady's face.
And (so shall ye know that she
Dwelleth in loftier light than we,
As intimate with skyey things
As are creatures that have wings)
Being come to mountains seven,
Note that one that's nighest heaven:
Thereon lieth against the sun
A place of pleasaunce, all o'errun

With whisperous shade, and blossoming
Of divers trees, wherein do sing
The little birds, and all together,
All day long in happy weather.
And well I ween that since the birth
Of Adam's firstborn, not on earth
Hath ever been such sweet singing
Of bird on bough, as here doth bring
Into a large and leafy ease
His sense that strayeth among the trees,
Where mingled is full many a note
Of golden-finch and speckle-throat.
Even the hoarse-chested starling
Here, where creepeth never a snarling
Gust to vex his heart, all day
Learneth a more melodious lay
Than that whereby this bird is known,
Which, otherwhere, with chiding tone,
What time the fretful Spring doth heave
The frozen North, to winds, that grieve
Round about the grave of March,
He chaunteth from the cloudy larch:
The linnet loud, and throstle eke,
And the blackbird of golden beak,
With perpetual madrigals
Do melodise the warm green walls
Of those blossom-crownèd groves,
In whose cool hearts the cooing doves
Make murmurings innumerable,
Of sound as sweet as when a well
With noise of bubbled water leapeth
At a green couch where Silence sleepeth:
Nor less, the long-voiced nightingale
Doth, deep down in bloomy vale
Delicious, pour at full noonlight

The song he hath rehearsed o'er-night;
And many other birds be there
Of most sweet voice, and plumage rare,
And names that I not know.   Of trees
That spring therein such plenty is
That I to tell them over all
Encumber'd am.   Both maple tall
There showeth his silver-mottled bark;
And beeches, colour'd like the dark
Red wine o' the South; and laurels green,
Sunny and smooth, that make rich screen
Round mossy places, where all day
Red squirrels and grey conies play,
Munching brown nuts and such wild fare
As tumbleth from the branches there.
And, for moisture of sweet showers,
All the grass is thick with flowers;
Primrose pure, that cometh alone;
Daisies quaint, with savour none,
But golden eyes of great delight,
That all men love, they be so bright;
And, cold in grassy cloister set,
Many a maiden violet;
The bramble flower, the scarlet hepe,
Hangeth above in sunny sleep;
And all around be knots and rows
Of tufted thyme, and lips of cows;
Whose sweet savour goeth about
The jocund bowers, in and out,
And dieth over all the place;
So that there is not any space
Of sun or shade, but haunted is
With ghosts of many sweetnesses.
There, dreading no intrusive stroke
Of lifted axe, the lusty oak

Broad his branches brown doth fling,
And reigneth, "every inch a king:"
Him also of that other kind
In great plenty shall ye find,
That while the great year goeth around
Sheddeth never his leaves to ground,
But in himself his summer hath,
And oweth not, nor borroweth,
As (though but rare) there be some wise
Good men, that to themselves suffice;
But in northern land we see
Full few, and they but stunted be,
Of this goodly kind of tree.
The ever-trembling birch, through all
Her hoary lights ethereal,
Doth twinkle there, 'twixt green and grey;
And of fruit-trees is great array:
The apple and the pear tree both,
Smother'd o'er in creamy froth
Of bubbled blossoms; the green fig,
With leathern leaves, and horny twig,
And gluey globes; the juniper,
That smelleth sweet in midsummer;
Nor peach-tree, there, nor apricot,
Needeth either nail or knot;
Nor there from churlish weathers wince
The orange, lemon, plum, and quince;
But under these, by grassy slopes,
Hangeth the vine her leafy ropes;
Wild Proteus she, o' the wanton wood,
That ever shifteth her merry mood,
And, aye in luxury of change,
Loveth to revel, and dance, and range,
In leaves, not hers, she fleeteth through,
Hiding her large grape-bunches blue;

And here, o'er haunts he maketh brown
With droppings from his scented crown,
Standeth the stately sycamore,
Lifting airy terrace o'er
Airy terrace;—such of yore
Dusky masons, deftly skill'd
Mighty stones to pile and build,
Up-hung in sumptuous Babylon,
For silken kings at set of sun
To dally with dark girls; but these
Are humm'd about by honey bees,
And cicale all day long
Creek the chamber'd shades among.
Far away, down hills that seem
Liquid (for the light doth stream
Through and through them) like that vail
Of lucid mist Morn spreadeth pale
O'er Summer's sallow forehead, found
Somewhere asleep on upland ground
Under the shade of heavy woods,
Imaginary multitudes
Of melancholy olives waste
Their wanness, smiling half effaced
In a smooth sea of slumbrous glory;
But high on inland promontory
Blandly the broad-headed pine,
Basking in the blue divine,
Drowseth, drench'd with sunny sky:
And, while the blue needle-fly
Nimbly pricketh in and out
The leaf-broider'd lawns about,
(As busy she as highborn dame
In shining silk, at tambour frame),
The pomegranate, flowering flame,
Burneth lone in cool retreats,

Hidden from those gorgeous heats
Where summer smoldereth into sweets.
Now, when ye have this goodly wood
All roamèd through, in gamesome mood,
At morning tide, and thereon spent
Large wealth of love and wonderment,
In honour due of such full cheer
And lustihood as laugheth here
The well-bower'd grass about,
That windeth in, and windeth out,
Under those bright ribandings
The red-budded bramble flings
From branch to branch, still straying on
Softly, ye shall be ware anon
Of a fair garden, glad and great,
Where my Lady, in high state
Of beauty, doth 'twixt eve and noon,
Under a spiritual moon,
Visit full oft her vassal flowers
In silent and sweet-scented hours,
When quiet vast is everywhere,
About the blue benignant air
And the cool grass, a deep immense
Gladness, an undisturbèd sense
Of goodness in the gather'd calm
Of old green woodlands bathed in calm,
And bounteous silence. . . . O my love,
How softly do the sweet hours move
About thy peaceful perfectness!
O hasten, little Songs! O press
To meet my Lady, ye that be
Her children, if she knew! . . . But she
Still lingereth, and the silver dawn
Is silent on the unfooted lawn.
Here all day doth couch and sport

Trim Flora, with her florid court:
Roses that be illuminèd
With royal colour rich and red;
Some, with bosoms open wide,
Where the brown bee, undenied,
Drinketh deep of honey drops;
Others, whose enamell'd knops
Prettily do peep between
Their half-bursten cradles green;
Lordly lilies, pale and proud;
And of all flowers a great crowd;
Whose rare-colour'd kirtles show
More hues than of the rainy bow.
In sweet warmth and lucid air
Nod they all and whisper, where
Lightly along each leafy lane
Zephyrus, with his tripping train,
Cometh at cool of even hour
To greet in all her pomp and power
Queen Flora, when in mansions damp
Of the dim moss his spousal lamp
Aloof the enamour'd glow-worm doth
Softly kindle; while the moth
Flitteth; and, at elfin rites,
Sprucely dance the little Sprites
Under the young moon all alone,
Round about King Oberon.
But ye this pleasaunce fair shall reach
Ere yet from off the slanted peach
The drops of silver dew be slipp'd,
Or night-born buds be open-lipp'd,
There shall ye find, in lustrous shade
Of laurels cool, an old well-head
That whelmeth up from under-ground,
And falleth with a tinkling sound

In a broad basin, builded there,
All rose-porphyry, smooth and fair.
The water is ever fresh and new,
As that Narcissus gazed into,
When, for love of his sweet self,
He fainted from the flowery shelf,
Leaving Echo all that pain;
So that now there doth remain
Of him that was so fair and sweet
Only in some green retreat
A purple flower seldom found,
And of her a hollow sound
In hollow places.   There shall ye
Pause as ye pass, and sing . . "To thee,
Water, our Master bade us say
Glad be thy heart, and pure alway;
May thy full urn never fail;
Thee nor sun nor frost assail,
Nor wild winter's wind molest thee;
Never newt nor eft infest thee;
Taint nor trouble touch thee never;
Heaven above thee smile for ever;
Earth around thee ever bear
Beauteous buds and blossoms rare;
Far from thee be all foul things,
Slaves to thee be all sweet springs,
Because thou, of thy kindness, hast
Shown, in blissful summers past,
To fondest eyes have ever been,
Sweetest face was ever seen:
Therefore be blest for evermore."
But if, my Songs, ye would explore
This pleasaunce all, there be therein
Delights so many, day would win
His under-goal ere ye were forth

Of your much musing on the worth
That is therein, and wondrous grace:
Therefore, ere the sun down-pace,
Must ye onward, where is spread
A fair terrace; and overhead
Thick trellis of the trembling vine,
That with leaves doth loop and twine
Aëry casements, whence the glance
Of whoso there, as in a trance,
Walketh about the whisperous shade
Under that vaulted verdure laid,
Seëth far down, and far away,
Tower'd cities, throng'd and gay,
Blowing woodlands, bright blue streams
Sparkling outward, yellow gleams
Of wavèd corn, and sun-burnt swells
Of pasture, soothed with sounds of bells
Sprinkled in air, of various tone,
From little hillside chapels lone,
And peaceful flocks that stray and pass
Down endless lengths of lowland grass.
And, certes, I will boldly say
Of this fair place, let mock who may,
That of joy the quintessence
Hath never slept about the sense
Of mortal man that is to die
With fulness sweet as that which I
Deep in my solaced heart have known,
Whilom walking, not alone,
Here in summer morns and eves,
When shadowy showers of flittering leaves
Fell, shaken thick from many a rout
Of little birds that fast flew out
Above us; interruption sweet
To converse, felt the more complete

For the interposèd pauses
Born of all such innocent causes.

High on the happy lawn above
Standeth the dwelling of my love.
Fair white all the mansion seemeth,
Save where in green shadow dreameth
The broad blossom-buttress'd roof,
Or where the many-colour'd woof
Of honeysuckle and creeping flowers,
Visibly from vernal showers
Winning length, hath broider'd all
With braided buds the southern wall.
Therein many windows be ;
And every window fair to see,
O'er-canopied with hangings bright,
For shelter fresh from summer light. ˙
And underneath, in urns and pots,
Sweet-smelling basil, and red knots
Of roses ripe ; for every casement
Is balconied about at basement,
A space where three or four may sit
At interchange of song or wit,
In the low amber evening hours,
Overlooking lawns and flowers.
In the hall, which is beneath,
A fountain springeth and echoeth,
Blown by a sad-looking Nymph,
Ravisht from her native lymph
And mossy grot, in days of old ;
And in marble mute and cold
Here for ever must she dwell
Uncompanion'd, by the spell
Of a stern old sculptor caught ;

For, aye since then, the hand that wrought
This stony charm her limbs upon
May not undo it.   Years are gone,
And still about her doth she stare,
Amazed however she came there.

But ye, since ye be free to rove
This mansion through, to floors above
Up the majestic marble stair
Pass with still steps, unseen, to where
Soon shall ye find, in sequel long,
Twelve great chambers: some be hung
With arras quaint, that doth portray
Hounds that hold the hart at bay
In good green wood, and hunters bold,
And dames aclad in green and gold ;
And evermore their horns be wound,
And evermore there cometh no sound :
Others in glowing fresco tell
Great Cæsar's tale, and how he fell,
Pierced through and through; with many a story
Of ancient kings that be in glory,
And high-renownèd heroes old ;
Sir Tristram, with his harp of gold,
That rashly drain'd the philtre brew'd
By the witch Queen for fair Isoud ;
Roland in Roncesvallès slain;
And bold Sir Ogier the Dane;
Huon of Bordeaux, love's true star;
Saladin with his scimitar;
The Red-beard Kaiser, sleeping still
Hid in the heart of Salzburg Hill;
David that danceth round the ark;
And Charlemagne; ye there may mark.

But, O my Songs, more softly now,
More softly move! Breathe low, breathe low!
For, by my heart's most tender fear,
I know that ye must now be near
The place where, nesting meek and warm,
Rosy cheek on snowy arm,
With loos'd hair and lidded eye
Dreaming doth my Lady lie:
And all around the restful air
Is silent, sweet, and pure, as where
Fond hands some holy taper trim,
Peaceful in sacred precincts dim.
Now, that my spirit, though far away
From her loved beauty, night and day
Ever in unreleasèd pine
Seeking, on many a musèd line,
To flow toward her, purely may
Her pureness praise,—humbly I pray
Of all good things that wait upon
The mind that maketh devotion
To what is fair (since such do lean
O'er mortal spirits oft unseen
Out of the deep and starry night,
Or steal on beams of morning light,
Or breath of buds, or sound of song
Remember'd, to keep safe from wrong,
And wretchedness, and self-mistrust,
Whatever warreth in this dust
Against oblivion), that their grace
May from my spirit purge and chase
All that is in it not sweet and pure;
So may I look with insight sure
Into myself, and favour find
To make a mirror within my mind,
Whereon, unsoil'd of any taint

Of sinful thought, my most sweet saint
Her fairness may from far let fall
In a deep peace perpetual.

The memory of her is mellow light
In darkness, mingling something bright
With all things; like a summer night.

The presence of her is young sunrise,
That gladdeneth, and, in wondrous wise,
Glorifieth, the earth and skies:

Her spirit is tender and bright as dew
Of May-morn fresh, when stars be few:
Her heart is harmless, simple, and true,

And blithe, and sweet, as bird in bower,
That singeth alone from hour to hour:
Her face is fair as April flower:

Her voice is fresh as bubbling bound
Of silver stream, in land new found,
That maketh ever a pleasant sound

To the soul of a thirsty traveller:
Her laugh is light as grasshopper:
Her breath is sweet as midsummer:

Her hair is a marvellous living thing
With a will of its own: the little locks fling
Showers of brown gold, gambolling

Over the ever-fleeting shade
About her shoulder and sweet throat stray'd,
With delicate odours underlaid:

Like calm midsummer cloud, nor less
Clothed with sweet light and silentness,
She in her gracious movement is:

Noble withal, and free from fear
As heart of eagle, and high, and near
To heaven in all her ways: of cheer

Gentle, and meek, from harshness free
As heart of dove: nor chideth she
Things ill, but knoweth not that they be:

All clear as waters clean that run
Through shadow sweet, and through sweet sun,
Her pure thoughts are: scorn hath she none:

But in my Lady's perfect nature
All is sincere, and of sweet feature.
This earth hath none such other creature.

Rise, little Songs, on nimble wing!
Arise! arise! as larks do sing
Lost in that heaven of light they love,
So rise, so lose yourselves above
My darkness, in the perfect light
Of her that is so pure and bright!
Rise, little Songs! with lusty cheer

Rise up to greet my Lady dear.
Be bold, and say to her with pride,—
"We are the souls of loves that died;
Whose sweetness is hope sorrow-fed,
Whose tendernesses tears unshed;
And we are essences that rise
From passions burn'd in sacrifice;

The youngest and bright-eyèd heirs
Of blind unbeautiful despairs;
Voiced resignations, once dumb wrongs."
Then, if she smile on you, my Songs,
Say, as I bid you, word for word,
" Lady of him that is our lord,
We from his heart, where we were born,
Shelter'd, and shut from shame and scorn,
Now at his bidding (well-a-day
For him, and us !) being fled away,
Never again may there abide,
Never return, and, undenied,
Creep in, and fold our wings, and rest
At peace in our abandon'd nest.
Wherefore, dear mistress, prithee take
(By true love sent, for true love's sake)
To thy sweet heart, and spirit pure,
Us, that must else but ill endure
The scorns of time, and haply fare
Homeless as birds in winter are."

But if that, on your way to greet
My gracious Lady, ye should meet
Haply elsewhere with other folk
Who may ask ye in scorn or joke,—
" Pray you now, little Songs, declare
,Who is that lady so sweet and fair,
Whereof this singer that sent you sings,
As certainly sweeter than all sweet things? "
See that ye answer not, Songs, but deep
In your secretest hearts my secret keep;
Lest the world, that loveth me not, should tell
The name of the Lady I love so well.

———

SEA-SIDE ELEGIACS.

EVER my heart beateth high and the blood in me
  danceth delighted,
  When, in the wind on the wharf, keen from the edge
    of the land,
Watching the white-wingèd black-bodied ships, as they
    rise uninvited
  Over the violet-dark wall o' the waters, I stand.
Wondrous with life that is in them, aware of the waters
    and weathers,
  They to the populous port pass with a will of their
    own.
Merrily singeth the mariner there, as the cable he
    tethers
  Tight to the huge iron ring, hung in the green gluey
    stone.
Swept with the spray is the pavement above; and the
    sea-wind is salt there.
  Down on the causeys all day, humming, the mer-
    chants unlade
Marvellous merchandise, while the sea-engines of
    burthen, at halt there
  Shoulder each other, and loll, lazy in shine or in
    shade.
O for the wing o' the grey sea-eagle, that far away
    inland
  Croucheth in cave or in creek, waiting the wind on
    the height !
When night cometh, the great north-wind, blowing
    bleak over Finland,
  Leapeth, and, lifting aloft, beareth him into the night.
O for the wing o' the bird ! and O for the wind o' the
    ocean !

O for the far-away lands ! O for the faces unfound !
Would I were hence ! for my spirit is fill'd with a mighty
    emotion.
    Why must the spirit, though wing'd, thus to the body
      be bound?
Ah, but my heart sinketh low, and the rapturous vein is
    arrested,
    When, at the mid o' the night, high on the shadowy
      land,
Mournfully watching the ghost-white waves, livid-lipp'd,
    hollow-breasted,
    Sob over shingle and shell, here with my sorrow I
      stand. ·
Weary of woe that is in them, fatigued by the violent
    weathers,
    Feebly they tumble and toss, sadly they murmur and
      moan,
Coldly the moon looketh down through the wan-rolling
    vapour she gathers
    Silently, cloud after cloud, round her companionless
      throne.
Dark up above is the wharf; and the harbour. The
    night-wind alone there
Goeth about in the night, humming a horrible song.
Black misshapen bulks, coil'd cumbrous things, over-
    thrown there,
    Seem as, in sullen dismay, silently suffering wrong.
O for the wing o' the grey sea-eagle, roamer of heaven !
    Him doth the wind o' the night bear through the
      night on its breast.
Over the howling ocean, and unto his ancient haven,
    Far in the land that he loves finding the realms of his
      rest.
O for the wing o' the bird ! and O for the wind o' the
    Ocean !

O for the lands that are left ! O for the faces of eld!
Would I were hence ! for my spirit is fill'd with a mourn-
    ful emotion.
  Why must the spirit, though wing'd, still by the body
    be held ?

———

THE SHORE.

Can it be women that walk in the sea-mist, under the
    cliffs there
  Which the unsatisfied surge sucks with importunate
    lip ?
There, where out from the sand-chok'd anchors, on to
    the skiffs there,
  Twinkle the slippery ropes, swinging adip and adrip?
All the place in a lurid, glimmering, emerald glory,
  Glares like a Titan world come back under heaven
    again :
Yonder, aloof are the steeps of the sea-kings, famous in
    story ;
  But who are they on the beach? they are neither
    women nor men.
Who knows, are they the land's, or the water's, living
    creatures ?
  Born of the boiling sea? nurst in the seething storms?
With their woman's hair dishevell'd over their stern male
    features,
  Striding, bare to the knee; magnified maritime forms !
They may be the mothers and wives, they may be the
    sisters and daughters

Of men on the dark mid-seas, alone in those black
　　coil'd hulls,
That toil 'neath yon white cloud, whence the moon will
　　rise o'er the waters
　　To-night, with her face on fire, if the wind in the
　　　evening lulls.
But they may be merely visions, such as only sick men
　　witness,
　　(Sitting as I sit here, fill'd with a wild regret),
Framed from the sea's misshapen spume with a horrible
　　fitness
　　To the winds in which they walk, and the surges by
　　　which they are wet :—
Salamanders, sea-wolves, witches, warlocks; marine
　　monsters
　　Which the dying seaman beholds, when the rats are
　　　swimming away,
And an Indian wind 'gins hiss from an unknown isle,
　　and alone stirs
　　The broken cloud which burns on the verge of the
　　　dead, red day.
I know not.　All in my mind is confused; nor can I
　　dissever
　　The mould of the visible world from the shape of my
　　　thought in me.
The Inward and Outward are fused: and, through them,
　　murmur for ever
　　The sorrow whose sound is the wind, and the roar of
　　　the limitless sea.

———

THE VAMPIRE.

I.

I FOUND a corpse, with glittering hair,
  Of a woman whose face, tho' dead,
The white death in it had left still fair,
  Too fair for an earthly bed !
So I loosen'd each fold of her bright curls, roll'd
From forehead to foot in a gush of red gold,
  And kiss'd her lips till her lips were red,
And warm and light on her eyelids white
. I breath'd, and press'd unto mine her breast,
  Till the blue eyes oped, and the breast grew warm.
And this woman, behold ! arose up bold,
  And, lifelike lifting a wilful arm,
With steady feet from the winding sheet
  Stepp'd forth to a mutter'd charm.

II.

And now beside me, whatever betide me,
  This woman is, night and day.
For she cleaves to me so, that, wherever I go
  She is with me the whole of the way.
And her eyes are so bright in the dead of the night,
  That they keep me awake with dread ;
While my life-blood pales in my veins, and fails,
  Because her red lips are so red
That I fear 'tis my heart she must eat for her food ;
  And it makes my whole flesh creep
To think she is drinking and draining my blood,
  Unawares, if I chance to sleep.

III.

It were better for me, ere I came nigh her,—
  This corpse,—ere I looked upon her,—
Had they burn'd my body in penal fire
  With a sorcerer's dishonour.
For, when the devil hath made his lair
  In the living eyes of a dear dead woman,
(To bind a man's strength by her golden hair,
  And break his heart, if his heart be human),
Is there any penance, or any prayer,
  That may save the sinner whose soul he tries
To catch in the curse of the constant stare
  Of those heartbreaking bewildering eyes,—
Comfortless, cavernous glowworms that glare
  From the gaping grave where a dead hope lies?
It is more than the soul of a man may bear.
  For the misery worst of all miseries
Is Desire eternally feeding Despair
  On the flesh, or the blood, that forever supplies
Life more than enough to keep fresh in repair
  The death ever dying, which yet never dies.

A REMONSTRANCE.

I.

Deem, if thou wilt, that I am all, and worse
  Than all, they bid thee deem that I must be.
But, ah! wilt thou desert love's universe,
  Deserting me?

II.

Not for my sake, be mine unworth forgiven,
  But for thine own. Since I, despite my dearth
Of all that made thee, what thou art, my Heaven,
  Am still thine Earth;

III.

Still thy love's only habitable star;
  Whose element engender'd, and embosoms
All thoughts, all feelings, all desires, which are
  Love's roots and blossoms.

IV.

Who will hold dear the ashes of the days
  Burn'd out on altars deem'd no more divine?
Rests there of thy soul's wealth enough to raise
  A new god's shrine?

V.

Who will forgive thy cheek its faded bloom,
  Save he whose kisses that blanch'd rose hath fed
Thine eyes, the stain of tears—save he for whom
  Those tears were shed?

VI.

Despite the blemisht beauty of thy brow,
  Thou would'st be lonely could'st thou love again;
For love renews the beautiful. But thou
  Hast only pain.

VII.

How wilt thou bear from pity to implore
　　What once thy power from rapture could command?
How wilt thou stretch—who wast a Queen of yore—
　　A suppliant's hand?—

VIII.

Even of thy pride be poor enough to ask
　　Love's purchased shelter, charitably chill,
Yet hast thou strength to recommence the task
　　Of pardoning still?

IX.

For who will prize in thee love's loss of all
　　Love hath to give save pardon for love wrong'd,
Unless that pardon be, whate'er befall
　　Love's pride, prolong'd?

X.

And thou—to whom demanding all that I
　　Can claim no more, wilt thou henceforth extend
Forgiveness on forgiveness, with that sigh
　　Which shuns the end?

XI.

Where wilt thou find the unworthier lips than mine
　　To plead for pardon with a prayer more lowly?
To whom else, pardoning much, become divine
　　By pardoning wholly?—

XII.

Ah, if thy heart can pardon yet, why yet
  Should not its latest pardon be for me?
And, if thou *will not* pardon, canst thou set
  Thy future free

XIII.

From the unpardon'd past, and so forget me?
  If not,—forgive me for thine own sad sake;
Else, having left me, thou would'st still regret me,
  And still would'st take

XIV.

Revenge for that regret on thine own bosom,
  Revenge on others for the failure, found
In them, to rear transplanted love to blossom
  On blighted ground.

XV.

As lion, tho' by lion wounded, still
  Doth miss the boisterous pastime of his kind,
Or wild sea-eagle, though with broken quill,
  Clipt, and confined,

XVI.

And fed on dainty fare among the doves,
  Doth miss the stormy sea-wind and the brine,
So would'st thou miss, amid all worthier loves,
  The unworth of mine.

XVII.

Then, if the flush of love's first faith be wan,
　　And thou wilt love again, again love me,
For what I am—no Saint, but still a man
　　That worships thee.

MEETING AGAIN.

I.

Yes, I remember the white rose.　And, since then, the
　　young ivy has grown,
From your window we could not reach it, and now it is
　　over the stone.
It was yonder that I first met you.　Well, time hath his
　　own stern cures!
And Alice's eyes are deeper, and her hair has grown like
　　yours.

II.

Your voice, too,—that is alter'd.　But there's something
　　here amiss
When it is not well to speak kindly.　And the olives are
　　ripe, by this.
I had fancied, and fear'd . . . but it matters not!　That
　　was my fault, I suppose.
Good-night! it is night so soon now.　Look there, you
　　have dropp'd your rose.

III.

Nay, I have one that is wither'd, and dearer to me. I came
To say good-night, little Alice. She does not remember
    my name !
It is but the heat that is making my head and my heart
    ache so.
I never was strong in the old time, as the others were,
    you know.

IV.

Is it late? is it late, Irene? The old name sounds so
    dear !
'Tis the last time I shall use it. You need show neither
    anger nor fear.
Good-night, good-night, little Alice ! Nay, lady, I need
    no light.
I remember the road, and I noticed the road is unalter'd.
    Good-night !

EARTH'S HAVINGS.

(SONG.)

WEARY the cloud falleth out of the sky,
    Dreary the leaf lieth low.
All things must come to the earth by-and-by,
    Out of which all things grow.

Let the wild wind laugh and whistle
 Aloof in the lonesome wood :
In our garden let the thistle
 Start where the rose-tree stood :
Let the rotting moss fall rotten
 With the rain-drops from the eaves:
Let the dead past lie forgotten
 In his grave with the yellow leaves.

Weary the cloud falleth out of the sky,
 Dreary the leaf lieth low.
All things must come to the earth by-and by,
 Out of which all things grow.

And again the hawthorn pale
 Shall blossom sweet i' the Spring :
And again the nightingale
 In the deep blue nights shall sing :
And seas of the wind shall wave
 In the light of the golden grain :
But the love that is gone to his grave
 Shall never return again.

Weary the cloud falleth out of the sky,
 Dreary the leaf lieth low
All things must come to the earth by-and-by,
 Out of which all things grow.

———

THE LAST FAREWELL.

I.

Away! away! in those wild eyes
    Repress the tears whose right is o'er
To flow for me.   Wrung hands, and sighs,
    And self-rebukes can not restore
        What is no more.

II.

Vain are all words, all weepings vain!
    We met too soon: we part too late.
Still wear, as best thou can'st, the chain
    Thine own hands forged about thy fate,
        Who could'st not wait.

III.

Be happy!   Haunt where music plays,
    And find no pain in music's tone.
Be fair!   Nor blush when others praise
    That beauty, scarcely now thine own.
        What's done is done.

IV.

Take, if thou can'st, from off thy youth
    The mark of mine, which burns there yet.
Take from that unremembering mouth
    The seal which there mine own hath set.
        And so, forget,

V.

Tho' unforgot !   It is thy doom
　To bear henceforth the heavy weight
Of my forgiveness to the tomb.
　I cannot save thee from thy fate;
　　Nor reinstate

VI.

Thy ruin'd pride, till in my grave
　Love's broken bond shall buried be.
And I, that would have died to save
　Thy heart's lost freedom, may not free
　　This load from thee.

VII.

Farewell, till life's mistake is over!
　When downward doth thy Genius turn
His wasted torch, and half uncover
　The date upon the funeral urn,
　　I will return.

VIII.

Then in the dark, the doubt, the fear,
　Amid the Spirits come to take thee,
Shall mine to thine again be near,
　And life's forgiveness mine shall make thee,
　　When death doth wake thee.

THE LAST ASSURANCE.

I.

FEAR me no more.   The last wild words are spoken.
  What heart have I, who worship'd once, to blame
    thee?
Never shall word or deed of mine betoken
The bond 'twixt thee and me which thou hast broken.
  In the lone years to come my lips shall name thee
    Never, child, never!

II.

And, if unprized applause, or scorned aspersion
  Should waft mine own name to thine ears again,
Know I have triumph'd,—not by thine exertion,
Or fail'd,—but not from thy forgiven desertion.
  For every link is lost between us twain,
    Forever, child, forever!

THE DESERTED PALACE.

I.

BROKEN are the Palace windows,
  Rotting is the Palace floor,
And the damp wind thro' the arras
  Sighs, and swings the creaking door.
But it only starts the white owl
  Perch'd upon a monarch's throne,
And the hungry rat that's gnawing
  Harpstrings tuneless every one.

II.

Dare you linger here at nightfall,
  When the hornèd owls do shout,
And the bat, the newt, the viper,
  And the dead men's ghosts come out?
Peep not, curious fool! nor enter ·
  Here where nobler things have been.
Lest you find a Phantom, sitting
  Throned where sat, long since, a Queen.

THE BURIED HEART.

THIS heart, you would not have,
I laid up in a grave
Of song: with love enwound it,
And set wild fancies blowing round it.

Then I to others gave it;
Because you would not have it.

"See you keep it well," I said,
"This heart's sleeping—is not dead—
But will wake some future day.
Keep and guard it while you may."

All great Sorrows,—sceptred some,
With gold crowns upon their heads,
Others that bare-footed roam,
Sadly telling cypress beads,

Pilgrims with no settled home,
Poorly clad in Palmer's weeds,
These from dismal dongeons come,
Faint and wan for want of food,
Those by many a bitter dart
From lost battlefields pursued,
—Each one clad in his own mood
Each one claiming his own part,—
A forlorn and famisht brood,—
Came to take my heart.

Then, in holy ground they set it,
With melodious weepings wet it,
And revered it, as they found it,
With wild fancies blowing round it.

And this heart (you would not have)
Being not dead, though in the grave,
Work'd miracles and marvels strange,
And heal'd many maladies :
Giving sight to seal'd-up eyes,
And legs to lame men sick for change.

The fame of it grew great and greater.
Then did you bethink you, later,
" How hath this heart, I would not take,
—This weak heart, a child might break—
Such glory gotten ?   Me he gave it :
Mine this heart, and I will have it."

Ah, too late ! For crowds exclaim'd
" Ours 'tis now : and hath been claim'd.
Moreover, where it lies, the spot
Is holy ground : so enter not

None but men of mournful mind—
Men to darken'd days resign'd;
Equal scorn of Saint and Devil;
Poor and outcast; halt and blind;
Exiles from Life's golden revel;
Gnawing at the bitter rind
Of old griefs ; or else, confined
In proud cares, to serve and grind—
May enter: whom this heart shall cure.
But go thou by: thou art not poor:
Nor defrauded of thy lot.
Bless thyself: but enter not ! "

———

HOW THESE SONGS WERE MADE.

I.

I SAT low down, at midnight, in a vale
  Mysterious with the silence of blue pines:
White-cloven by a snaky river-tail,
  Uncoil'd from tangled wefts of silver twines.

II.

Out of a crumbling castle, on a spike
  Of splinter'd rock, a mile of changeless shade
Gorged half the landscape.   Down a dismal dyke
  Of black hills the sluiced moonbeams stream'd, and
    staid.

III.

I pluck'd blue mugwort, livid mandrakes, balls
   Of blossom'd nightshade, heads of hemlock, long
White grasses, grown by mountain pedestals,
   To make ingredients fit, for many a song

IV.

Of fragrant sadness,—to embalm the Past—
   The corpse-cold Past—that it should not decay;
But in dark vaults of Memory, to the last,
   Endure unchanged: for in some future day

V.

I will bring my new love to look at it
   (Laying aside her gay robes for a moment)
That, seeing what love came to, she may sit
   Silent awhile, and muse, but make no comment.

———

THE PORTRAIT.

The man who told this tale is not
* Either you, or I, good friend;*
Who may therefore, glad of our better lot,
* Hear his story told to the end.*

I.

MIDNIGHT past! Not a sound of aught
   Thro' the silent house, but the wind at his prayers.
I sat by the dying fire, and thought
   Of the dear dead woman upstairs.

THE PORTRAIT.

II.

A night of tears! for the gusty rain
   Had ceased, but the eaves dripping yet;
And the moon look'd forth, as tho' in pain,
   With her face all white and wet:

III.

Nobody with me, my watch to keep,
   But the friend of my bosom, the man I love:
And grief had sent him fast to sleep
   In the chamber up above.

IV.

Nobody else, in the country place
   All round, that knew of my loss beside,
But the good young Priest with the Raphael-face
   Who confess'd her when she died.

V.

That good young Priest is of gentle nerve,
   And my grief had moved him beyond controul;
For his lip grew white, as I could observe,
   When he speeded her parting soul.

VI.

I sat by the dreary hearth alone:
   I thought of the pleasant days of yore:
I said "the staff of my life is gone:
   The woman I love is no more.

VII.

"Gem-clasp'd, on her bosom my portrait lies,
  Which next to her heart she used to wear—
It is steep'd in the light of her loving eyes,
  And the sweets of her bosom and hair."

VIII.

And I said—"the thing is precious to me:
  They will bury her soon in the churchyard clay;
It lies on her heart, and lost must be,
  If I do not take it away."

IX.

I lighted my lamp at the dying flame,
  And crept up the stairs that creak'd for fright,
Till into the chamber of death I came,
  Where she lay all in white.

X.

The moon shone over her winding sheet.
  There, stark she lay on her carven bed:
Seven burning tapers about her feet,
  And seven about her head.

XI.

As I stretch'd my hand, I held my breath;
  I turn'd, as I drew the curtains apart:
I dared not look on the face of death:
  I knew where to find her heart.

XII.

I thought, at first, as my touch fell there,
    It had warm'd that heart to life, with love;
For the thing I touch'd was warm, I swear,
    And I could feel it move.

XIII.

'Twas the hand of a man, that was moving slow
    O'er the heart of the dead,—from the other side:
And at once the sweat broke over my brow,
    " Who is robbing the corpse?" I cried.

XIV.

Opposite me, by the tapers' light,
    The friend of my bosom, the man I loved,
Stood over the corpse, and all as white,
    And neither of us moved.

XV.

" What do you here, my friend?" . . . The man
    Look'd first at me, and then at the dead.
" There is a portrait here . . ." he began;
    " There is.   It is mine," I said.

XVI.

Said the friend of my bosom, "yours, no doubt,
    The portrait was, till a month ago,
When this suffering angel took that out,
    And placed mine there, I know."

XVII.

" This woman, she loved me well," said I.
  " A month ago," said my friend to me :
" And in your throat," I groan'd, " you lie ! "
  He answer'd . . . "let us see."

XVIII.

" Enough ! " I return'd, " let the dead decide :
  And whose soever the portrait prove,
His shall it be, when the cause is tried,
  Where Death is arraign'd by Love."

XIX.

We found the portrait, there in its place :
  We open'd it by the tapers' shine :
The gems were all unchanged : the face
  Was—neither his nor mine.

XX.

" One nail drives out another, at least !
  The portrait is not ours," I cried,
" But our friend's, the Raphael-faced young Priest,
  Who confess'd her when she died."

———

GOING BACK AGAIN.

I.

I DREAM'D that I walk'd in Italy,
    When the day was going down,
By a water that silently wander'd by
    Thro' an old dim-lighted town,

II.

Till I come to a palace fair to see.
    Wide open the windows were.
My love at a window sat; and she
    Beckon'd me up the stair.

III.

I roam'd thro' many a corridor,
    And many a chamber of state:
Dim and silent was every floor,
    And the day was growing late.

IV.

When I came to the little rose-colour'd room
    From the curtains outflew a bat.
The window was open: and in the gloom
    My love at the window sat.

V.

She sat with her guitar on her knee,
    But she was not singing a note,
For some one had drawn (ah, who could it be?)
    A knife across her throat.

TWO OUT OF THE CROWD.

I.

ONE circle of all its golden hours
  The flitting hand of the timepiece there,
In its close white bower of china flowers,
  Hath rounded unaware:

II.

While the firelight, flung from the flickering wall
  On the large and limpid mirror behind,
Hath redden'd and darken'd down o'er all,
  As the fire itself declined.

III.

Something of pleasure, and something of pain
  There lived in that sinking light.   What is it?
Faces I never shall look at again,
  In places you never will visit,

IV.

Reveal'd themselves from each faltering ember,
  While, under a palely-wavering flame,
Half of the years life aches to remember
  Reappear'd and died as they came.

V.

To its dark Forever an hour hath gone
  Since either you or I have spoken:
Each of us might have been sitting alone
  In a silence so unbroken.

VI.

I never shall know what made me look up
  (In this cushion'd chair so soft and deep,
By the table where, over the empty cup,
  I was leaning, half asleep)

VII.

To catch a gleam on the picture up there
  Of the saint in the wilderness under the oak:
And a light on the brow of the bronze Voltaire,
  Like the ghost of a cynical joke;

VIII.

To mark, in each violet, velvet fold
  Of the curtains that fall 'twixt room and room,
The drowsy flush of the red light roll'd
  Thro' their drapery's glowing gloom.

IX.

O'er the Rembrandt there—the Caracci here—
  Flutter warmly the ruddy and wavering hues;
And St. Anthony over his book has a leer
  At the little French beauty by Greuze.

X.

There—the Leda, weigh'd over her white swan's
    back,
  By the weight of her passionate kiss, ere it falls;
On the ebony cabinet, glittering black
  Thro' its ivory cups and balls:

XI.

Your scissors and thimble, and work laid away,
　　With its silks, in the scented rose-wood box;
The journals, that tell truth every day,
　　And that novel of Paul de Kock's:

XII.

The flowers in the vase, with their bells shut close
　　In a dream of the far green fields where they grew;
The cards of the visiting people and shows
　　In that bowl with the sea-green hue.

XIII.

Your shawl, with a queenly droop of its own,
　　Hanging over the arm of the crimson chair:
And, last—yourself, as silent as stone,
　　In a glow of the firelight there!

XIV.

I thought you were reading all this time.
　　And was it some wonderful page of your book
Telling of love, with its glory and crime,
　　That has left you that sorrowful look?

XV.

For a tear from those dark, deep, humid orbs,
　　'Neath their lashes, so long, and soft, and sleek,
All the light in your lustrous eyes absorbs,
　　As it trembles over your cheek.

XVI.

Were you thinking how we, sitting side by side,
　　Might be dreaming miles and miles apart?
Or if lips could meet over a gulf so wide
　　As separates heart from heart?

XVII.

Ah, well! when time is flown, how it fled
　　It is better neither to ask nor tell.
Leave the dead moments to bury their dead.
　　Let us kiss and break the spell!

XVIII.

Come, arm in arm, to the window here;
　　Draw the thick curtain, and see how, to-night,
In the clear and frosty atmosphere,
　　The lamps are burning bright.

XIX.

All night, and for ever, in yon great town,
　　The heaving Boulevart flares and roars;
And the streaming Life flows up and down
　　From its hundred open doors.

XX.

It is scarcely so cold, but I and you,
　　With never a friend to find us out,
May stare at the shops for a moment or two,
　　And wander a while about.

XXI.

For when in the crowd we have taken our place,
  (—Just two more lives to the mighty street there !)
Knowing no single form or face
  Of the men and women we meet there,—

XXII.

Knowing, and known of, none in the whole
  Of that crowd all round, but our two selves only,
We shall grow nearer, soul to soul,
  Until we feel less lonely.

XXIII.

Here are your bonnet and gloves, dear.   There—
  How stately you look in that long rich shawl !
Put back your beautiful golden hair,
  That never a curl may fall.

XXIV.

Stand in the firelight . . . so, . . . as you were—
  Oh my heart, how fearfully like her she seem'd !
Hide me up from my own despair,
  And the ghost of a dream I dream'd !

BLUEBEARD.

I.

FAIR in the love of Fatima
  (A maiden like an evening star)
Lay hid this stain'd and crookèd life,
  As in its sheath my scimitar:

II.

For fair with flow'rets damascene
  The sheath is traced and twined about,
But on the blade are blood-spots black
  That time and rust will not wear out.

III.

Beneath the hot pomegranate boughs
  At sunset here alone we sat.
To call back something from that hour,
  I'd give away my Caliphat.

IV.

"—Am I not fair?"
                    " As evening air,"
  I answer'd.
          " Fresh?"
                  " As April's sky."
" Whate'er I be," she whisper'd me,
  " I love thee, and all thine am I."

V.

" Be satisfied."
         " Alas ! " I sigh'd.
And " wherefore dost thou sigh ? " she said.
" Because I trace in thy fair face
    The likeness of a face that's dead."

VI.

Rash question, rash reply !
         The rest
    Is writ in tears where all who read
Revile my name. Ah Fatima,
    Why did'st thou seek to know my dead ?

VII.

Large realms were thine, with one reserve
    Full many a chamber, many a hall,
Thy wandering thought was free to rove :
    I gave thee up the keys of all.

VIII.

One only key I warn'd thee, spare
    To use ; because it opes a door
That's shut for thy sake and for mine,
    But, open'd once, will shut no more :

IX.

And thou that door hast oped, and thou
    Hast gazed upon the dead, and I
That most thy fault, rash child, deplore,
    Must needs inflict its penalty !

FATIMA.

I.

A YEAR ago, thy cheek was bright
  As oleander buds that break
The dark of yonder dells by night
  Above the lamplit lake.

II.

Pale as a snowdrop in Cashmere
  Thy face to-night, fair infant, seems.
Ah, wretched child ! what dost thou hear,
  When I talk in my dreams ?—

———

RESURRECTION.

I.

AT Paris it was, at the Opera there ;—
  And she look'd like a Queen of old time that night,
With the wreathèd pearls in her raven hair,
  And her breast with the diamond bright.

II.

Side by side in our box we sat,
  Together, my bride betroth'd and I :
My gaze was fix'd on my opera-hat,
  And hers on the stage hard by :

III.

And both were silent, and both were sad.
  Queenly she lean'd on her full white arm,
With that regal, indolent air she had ;
  So confident of her charm !

IV.

I have not a doubt she was thinking then
  Of her former lord, good soul that he was,
Who died the richest, and roundest of men,
  The Marquis of Carabas.

V.

That narrow gate to the kingdom of heaven,
  He was not too portly, I trust, to pass.
I wish him well, for the jointure given
  To my lady of Carabas.

VI.

Meanwhile, I was thinking of my first love,
  As I had not been thinking of aught for years,
Till over mine eyes there began to move
  Something that felt like tears.

VII.

I thought of the dress that she wore last time,
  When we stood, 'neath the cypress tree together,
In that lost land, in her own soft clime,
  In the crimson evening weather,

VIII.

By the broken wall, on the brown grass plot;
   And her warm white neck in its golden chain:
And her full, soft hair, wound into a knot,
   And falling loose again:

IX.

And the jasmin-flower in her fair young breast,
   (O the faint sweet smell of that jasmin-flower !)
And the last bird singing alone to his nest,
   And the first star over the tower.

X.

I thought of our little quarrels and strife,
   And the letter that brought me back my ring.
And it all seem'd then—in the waste of life—
   Such a very little thing !

XI.

For I thought of her grave below the hill,
   Which the sentinel cypress tree stands over.
And I thought . . . " were she only living still,
   How I could forgive her, and love her !"

XII.

And I swear, as I thought of her thus, in that hour,
   And of how, after all, old things were best,
That I smelt the smell of that jasmin-flower
   Which she used to wear in her breast.

XIII.

It smelt so faint, and it smelt so sweet,
  It made me creep, and it made me cold !
Like the scent that steals from the crumbling sheet
  Where a mummy is half unroll'd.

XIV.

And I turn'd and look'd. She was sitting there
  In a dim box over the stage; and drest
In the dress that I knew,—with that full soft hair,
  And that jasmin in her breast.

XV.

She was there, and I was here :
  And the glittering horseshoe curved between;
And from here to there, and from tier to tier,
  —From my bride that was to have been,

XVI.

To my early love, with her eyes down-cast,
  And over her blush-rose face the shade,
(In short, from the Future back to the Past)
  There was but a step to be made.

XVII.

To my early love from my future bride
  One moment I look'd. Then I stole to the door,
And traversed the passage, and down at her side
  I was sitting a moment more.

XVIII.

My thinking of her, or the music's strain,
  Or something that never will be exprest,
Had brought her back from the grave again
  And brought her back to my breast.

XIX.

She is not dead, and she is not wed!
  But she loves me now, and she loved me then!
And the very first words that her sweet lips said,
  My heart grew youthful again.

XX.

The Marchioness there, of Carabas,
  She is wealthy, and young, and handsome still,
And but for her . . . well, we'll let that pass,
  She may marry whomever she will.

XXI.

But I will marry my own first love,
  With her blush-rose face : for old things are best;
And the flower in her bosom, I prize it above
  The brooch in my lady's breast.

XXII.

The world is fill'd with folly and sin,
  And love must cling where it can, I say:
For Beauty is easy enough to win ;
  But one isn't loved every day.

XXIII.

And I think, in the lives of most women and men,
  There's a moment when all would go smooth and
      even,
If only the dead could find out when
  To come back, and be forgiven.

THE CHESS-BOARD.

IRENE, do you yet remember,
  Ere we were grown so sadly wise,
Those evenings in the bleak December,
Curtain'd warm from the snowy weather,
When you and I play'd chess together,
  Checkmated by each other's eyes?
  Ah, still I see your soft white hand
Hovering warm o'er Queen and Knight.
  Brave Pawns in valiant battle stand:
The double Castles guard the wings:
The Bishop, bent on distant things,
Moves, sidling, through the fight.
  Our fingers touch: our glances meet,
  And falter; falls your golden hair
  Against my cheek; your bosom sweet
Is heaving. Down the field, your Queen
Rides slow her soldiery all between,
  And checks me unaware.
  Ah me! the little battle's done,
Disperst is all its chivalry;
Full many a move, since then, have we

'Mid Life's perplexing chequers made,
And many a game with Fortune play'd,—
　　What is it we have won?
　　This, this at least—if this alone;—
That never, never, never more,
As in those old still nights of yore,
　　(Ere we were grown so sadly wise)
　　Can you and I shut out the skies,
Shut out the world, and wintry weather,
　　And, eyes exchanging warmth with eyes,
Play chess, as then we play'd, together!

FATA MORGANA.

I.

WHEN the latest strife is lost, and all is done with,
　　Ere we slumber in the spirit and the brain,
We drowse back, in dreams, to days that life begun with,
　　And their tender light returns to us again.

II.

I have cast away the tangle and the torment
　　Of the cords that bound my life up in a mesh:
And the pulse begins to throb that long lay dormant
　　'Neath their pressure; and the old wounds bleed afresh.

III.

I am touch'd again with shades of early sadness,
　　Like the summer-cloud's light shadow in my hair:
I am thrill'd again with breaths of boyish gladness,
　　Like the scent of some last primrose on the air.

IV.

And again she comes, with all her silent graces,
  The lost woman of my youth, yet unpossest:
And her cold face so unlike the other faces
  Of the women whose dead lips I since have prest.

V.

The motion and the fragrance of her garments
  Seem about me, all the day long, in the room:
And her face, with its bewildering old endearments,
  Comes at night, between the curtains, in the gloom.

VI.

When vain dreams are stirr'd with sighing, near the
      morning,
  To my own her phantom lips I feel approach:
And her smile, at eve, breaks o'er me without warning
  From its speechless, pale, perpetual reproach.

VII.

When Life's dawning glimmer yet had all the tint there
  Of the orient, in the freshness of the grass,
(Ah, what feet since then have trodden out the print
      there !)
  Did her soft, her silent footsteps fall, and pass.

VIII.

They fell lightly, as the dew falls, 'mid ungather'd
  Meadow-flowers; and lightly linger'd with the dew.
But the dew is gone, the grass is dried and wither'd,
  And the traces of those steps have faded too.

IX.

Other footsteps fall about me—faint, uncertain,
  In the shadow of the world, as it recedes:
Other forms peer thro' the half-uplifted curtain
  Of that mystery which hangs behind the creeds.

X.

What is gone is gone for ever.   And new fashions
  May replace old forms which nothing can restore:
But I turn from sighing back departed passions
  With that pining at the bosom as of yore.

XI.

I remember to have murmur'd, morn and even,
  " Though the Earth dispart these Earthlies, face from
    face,
Yet the Heavenlies shall surely join in Heaven,
  For the spirit hath no bonds in time or space:

XII.

" Where it listeth, there it bloweth; all existence
  Is its region; and it houseth, where it will.
I shall feel her through immeasurable distance,
  And grow nearer, and be gather'd to her, still.

XIII.

" If I fail to find her out by her gold tresses,
  Brows, and breast, and lips, and language of sweet
    strains,
I shall know her by the traces of dead kisses,
  And that portion of myself which she retains."

XIV.

But my being is confused with new experience,
   And changed to something other than it was;
And the Future with the Past is set at variance;
   And Life falters 'neath the burthens which it has.

XV.

Famisht hopes press fast behind me, weakly wailing:
   Faint before me fleets the good I have not done:
And my search for her may still be unavailing
   'Mid the spirits that are pass'd beyond the sun.

CONSOLATION.

WHEN I perceive how slight and poor appears
(Though with sad care and strong compulsion brought
Down rangèd rhymes with strenuous search of thought)
The express'd result of my most passionate years;
Remembering, too, from what divinest spheres
Stoop'd many a starry visitant, and taught
My spirit at her toils,—how round her wrought
Strong Raptures, Sorrows, Splendours rich in tears,
My whole heart fails me.   Then an inward voice
Replies, " Possess thyself, and be content.
Life's best is bound not by the utterance
Of any word, nor may in sound be spent,
To win back echoes out of hollow chance.
What thou hast *felt* is thine.   If much, rejoice."

A FOOTSTEP.

WITHIN my mind there is a garden : part
  Sprung from the greenest stray aways of Spring
  In a dewy time : part by long labouring
Of toilful Love, and many a culturing art
Learn'd of skill'd Grief in patientness of heart,
  Nor without weariness, wrought. Deep-blossoming
  Growths of long-planted pain cold shadow fling,
Sun-proof to every casual golden dart,
Over one aspect of this haunt.   Elsewhere
  Full sunlight sleeps for ever.   Many a day
I lose myself about this quiet place,
  Following one footstep ever the same way.
Dear, 'tis thy ghostly footstep that I trace,
  But thee thyself I find not here nor there.

REQUIESCAT.

I SOUGHT to build a deathless monument
  To my dead love.   Therein I meant to place
All precious things, and rare : as Nature blent
  All single sweetnesses in one sweet face.
I could not build it worthy her mute merit,
  Nor worthy her white brows and holy-eyes,
Nor worthy of her perfect and pure spirit,
  Nor of my own immortal memories.
But, as some rapt artificer of old,
  To enshrine the ashes of a virgin saint,
Might scheme to work with ivory, and fine gold,
  And carven gems, and legended and quaint
Seraphic heraldies; searching far lands,
  Orient and occident, for all things rare,
To consecrate the toil of reverent hands,
  And make his labour, like her virtue, fair ;
Knowing no beauty beautiful as she,
  And all his labour void, but to beguile
A sacred sorrow ; so I work'd.   Ah, see
  Here are the fragments of my shatter'd pile !
I keep them, and the flowers that sprang between
  Their broken workmanship—the flowers and
      weeds !
Sleep soft among the violets, O my Queen,
  Lie calm among my ruin'd thoughts and deeds !

MADAME LA MARQUISE.

I.

THE folds of her wine-dark violet dress
    Glow over the sofa fall on fall,
As she sits in the air of her loveliness,
    With a smile for each and for all.

II.

Half of her exquisite face in the shade,
    Which o'er it the screen in her soft hand flings;
Through the gloom glows her hair in its odorous braid;
    In the firelight are sparkling her rings.

III.

As she leans—the slow smile half shut up in her eyes,
    Beams the silky, long silk soft lashes beneath;
Through her crimson lips, stirred by her faint replies,
    Breaks one gleam of her pearl-white teeth.

IV.

As she leans—where your eye, by her beauty subdued,
    Droops—from under warm fringes of broidery white—
The slightest of feet, silken-slippered, protrude
    For one moment, then slip out of sight.

V.

As I bend o'er her bosom to tell her the news,
    The faint scent of her hair, the approach of her cheek,
The vague warmth of her breath, all my senses suffuse
    With HERSELF; and I tremble to speak.

VI.

As she sits in the curtained, luxurious light
    Of that room with its porcelain, and pictures, and
        flowers,
When the dark day's half done, and the snow flutters
        white
    From the windows in feathery showers,

VII.

All without is so cold—'neath the low leaden sky!
    Down the bald, empty street, like a ghost the gen-
        darme
Stalks surly; a distant carriage hums by,
    All within is so bright and so warm.

VIII.

Here we talk of the schemes and the scandals of court,
    How the courtesan pushes; the charlatan thrives;
We put horns on the heads of our friends, just for sport,
    Put intrigues in the heads of their wives.

IX.

Her warm hand, at parting, so strangely thrilled mine,
    That at dinner I scarcely remark what they say,
Drop the ice in my soup, spill the salt in my wine,
    Then go yawn at my favourite play.

X.

But she drives after noon:—then's the time to behold her,
    With her fair face half hid, like a ripe peeping rose,
'Neath that veil; o'er the velvets and furs which enfold
        her,
    Leaning back with a queenly repose.

XI.

As she glides up the sunlight !—you'd say she was made,
 To loll back in a carriage, all day with a smile,
And at dusk, on a sofa, to lean in the shade
 Of soft lamps, and be woo'd for awhile.

XII.

Could we find out her heart through that velvet and lace;
 Can it beat without ruffling her sumptuous dress;
She will show us her shoulder, her bosom, her face,
 But what the heart's like, we must guess.

XIII.

With live women and men to be found in the world—
 Live with sorrow and sin, live with pain and with
 passion—
Who could live with a doll, tho' its locks should be
 curled,
 And its petticoats trimmed in the fashion ?

XIV.

'Tis so fair !—would my bite, if I bit it draw blood ?
 Will it cry if I hurt it ? or scold if I kiss ?
Is it made, with its beauty of wax or of wood ?
 Is it worth while to guess at all this ?

———

MIDGES.

I.

She is talking æsthetics, the dear clever creature;
Upon man and his functions she speaks with a smile,
Her ideas are divine upon Art, upon Nature,
The Sublime, the Heroic, and Mr. Carlyle.

II.

I no more am found worthy to join in the talk, now,
So I follow with my surreptitious cigar,
Whilst she leads our poetical friend up the walk now,
Who quotes Wordsworth and praises her "Thoughts
on a Star!"

III.

Meanwhile, there is dancing in yonder green bower,
A swarm of young midges. They dance high and low,
'Tis a sweet little species that lives but an hour,
And the eldest was born half an hour ago.

IV.

One impulsive young midge, I hear ardently pouring,
In the ears of a shy little wanton in gauze,
His eternal devotion; his ceaseless adoring,
Which shall last till the universe breaks from its laws.

V.

His passion is not, he declares, the mere fever
Of a rapturous moment. It knows no control;
It will burn in his breast through existence for ever,
Immutably fixed in the deeps of his soul.

VI.

She wavers—she flutters—male midges are fickle,
    Dare she trust him her future?—she asks with a sigh,
He implores—and a tear is beginning to trickle,
    She is weak—they embrace and—the lovers pass by.

VII.

While they pass me—down here on a rose leaf has
        lighted
A pale midge, his feelers all drooping and torn,
His existence is withered; its future is blighted,
    His hopes are betrayed and his heart is forlorn.

VIII.

By the midge his heart trusted, his heart is deceived now,
    In the virtue of midges he no more believes
From love in its falsehood, once wildly believed now.
    He will bury his desolate life in the leaves.

IX.

His friends would console him—the noblest, sagest
    Of midges have held that a midge lives again;
In Eternity, say they, the strife thou now wagest
    With sorrow shall cease—but their words are in vain.

X.

Can eternity bring back the seconds now wasted
    In hopeless desire? or restore to his breast,
The belief he has lost, with the bliss he once tasted,
    Embracing the midge that his being loved best?

XI.

His friends would console him—the masses adore him:
　Many hundred long seconds he still has to live;
A beneficent public career is before him,
　Let him seek in the great world of action to strive!

XII.

There is Fame—there's Ambition! and grander than
　　either,
　There is Freedom—the progress and march of the race.
But to Freedom his breast beats no longer, and neither
　Ambition nor action her loss can replace.

XIII.

If the time had been spent in acquiring æsthetics
　I have squandered in learning this language of midges,
There might, for my friend in her peripatetics,
　Have been now two ones to help o'er the bridges.

XIV.

As it is, I'll report her the whole conversation.
　It would have been longer, but somehow or other
(In the midst of that misanthrope's long lamentation)
　A midge in my right eye became a young mother.

XV.

Since my friend is so clever, I'll ask her to tell me
　Why the least living thing (a mere midge in the egg!)
Can make a man's tears flow as now it befell me,
　Oh, you dear clever woman, explain it, I beg!

GOOD-NIGHT IN THE PORCH.

I.

A LITTLE longer in the light, love, let me be! The air
is warm.
I hear the cuckoo's last good-night float from the copse
below the Farm.
A little longer, Sister sweet—your hand in mine—on this
old seat!

II.

In yon red gable, which the rose creeps round and o'er,
your casement shines
Against the yellow west, o'er those few sinuous, melancholy pines.
The long, loud day is nearly done. How silent all the
place is grown!

III.

From the warm upland comes a gust made fragrant with
the brown hay there.
The meek cows, with their white horns thrust across
the hedge, stand still and stare.
The steaming horses from the wains droop o'er the tank
their plaited manes.

IV.

And o'er yon hill-side brown and barren (where you and
I, as children, play'd,
Starting the rabbit to his warren), I hear the sandy, shrill
cascade
Leap down upon the vale, and spill cool sound and light
i' the lonesome Mill.

V.

O can it be for nothing only that this fair world was
    shown to me?
Or but to leave the heart more lonely for loss of beauty?
    Can it be?
O closer, closer, Sister dear . . . nay, I have kist away
    that tear.

VI.

God bless you, for the tender thought which only upon
    tears could rise!
God bless you, for the love that sought to hide them in
    those drooping eyes,
Whose lids I kiss! . . . poor lids, so red! but let my
    kiss fall there instead.

VII.

Yes! sad, indeed, it seems each night,—and sadder,
    Sister, for your sake,—
To watch the last low lingering light, and know not
    where the morn may break.
To-night we sit together here. To-morrow night will
    come . . . ah, where?

VIII.

There's not a flower, there's not a tree, in this old garden
    where we sit,
But what some fragrant memory is closed and folded up
    in it.
To-night the dog-rose smells as wild, as fresh, as when I
    was a child!

IX.

'Tis eight years since (do you forget?) we set those lilies
    near the wall :
A blue-eyed infant, you! even yet I seem to see the
    ringlets fall—
The golden ringlets, blown behind your shoulders in the
    merry wind!

X.

Ah me! old times,—the sweet, the sting! And oft, by
    yonder green old gate
The field shows through, in morns of Spring, an eager
    boy, I paused elate
With all sweet fancies loosed from school. And oft, you
    know, when eves were cool

XI.

In August, bold as two young rooks perch'd in a belfry
    by themselves,
We, chatting of our favourite books, light-hearted over-
    weening elves,
Dealt praise or blame to poets gone, here in the wood-
    bine-porch alone.

XII.

Farewell, my epic—I began when life seem'd long,
    though longer art,—
And all the glorious deeds of man made golden riot in
    my heart—
Eight books . . . . it will not number nine! I die
    before my heroine.

XIII.

Sister ! they say that drowning men in one wild moment
    can recall
Their whole life long, and feel again the pain—the bliss
    —that throng'd it all.
Last night those phantoms of the past again came
    crowding round me fast.

XIV.

Near morning, when the lamp was low, against the wall
    they seem'd to flit;
And, as the wavering light would glow or fall, they
    came and went with it.
The ghost of boyhood seem'd to gaze down the dark
    verge of vanisht days.

XV.

Once more the garden, where she walk'd on summer
    eves to tend her flowers,
Once more the lawn, where first we talk'd of future
    years in twilight hours,
Arose ; once more she seem'd to pass before me, in the
    waving grass,

XVI.

To that old terrace ; her bright hair about her warm neck
    all undone,
And waving on the balmy air, with tinges of the dying
    sun ;
One lone bright star in the broad west ; one late bird
    singing near its nest.

XVII.

So lovely, so beloved! Oh fair as though that sun had
    never set
Which staid upon her golden hair, in dreams I seem to
    see her yet:
To see her in that old green place—the same husht
    smiling cruel face!

XVIII.

That hair, not unlike yours—as bright, but with a warmer
    golden tinge!
Those eyes, a somewhat deeper light, that dream'd
    beneath a longer fringe!
And still that strange grave smile she had stays in my
    soul and keeps it sad.

XIX.

From little things—a star, a flower—that touch'd us with
    the self-same thought,
My passion deepen'd hour by hour, until to such fierce
    heat 'twas wrought,
As, shrivelling over every nerve, crumbled the outworks
    of reserve.

XX.

I told her then, in that wild time, the love I knew she
    long had seen;
The accusing pain that burn'd like crime, yet left me
    nobler than I had been;
What matter with what words I woo'd her? She said I
    had misunderstood her.

XXI.

Misunderstood! misunderstood! . . . Ay, not her
    only, but thereby
All that souls say in flesh and blood! misunderstanding
    till I die
The meaning of that face, the while my heart lay aching
    in its smile.

XXII.

Misunderstood? misunderstood? ay, life, love, all things,
    when, alone,
I heard the crashing of my blood on the brute silence!
    She was gone.
The stinging sunlight stabb'd me through the leaves.
    Above, the blind, bright blue

XXIII.

Laugh'd, with no meaning, in my face. And nothing
    could I realise
Save a dull strangeness,—the disgrace of a stunn'd
    impotent surprise.
The great noon gaped: blithe birds were shrill. The
    world went on; my heart stood still.

XXIV.

My heart stands still, the world goes on, the years go by,
    and now a mild
Unmurmuring mind hath sorrow won from memory.
    I have seen her child,—
The self-same eyes its mother had,—that once had
    power to make me mad!

XXV.

Dark violet eyes whose glances, deep with April-hints of
  sunny tears,
'Neath long soft lashes laid asleep, seem'd all too
  thoughtful for her years !
As though from mine her gaze had caught the secret
  of some mournful thought.

XXVI.

But when she spake, her father's air broke o'er her . . .
  that clear confident voice !
Some happy souls there are that wear their nature
  lightly; these rejoice
The world by living, and receive from all men more
  than what they give.

XXVII.

One handful of their buoyant chaff excels our hoards of
  careful grain.
Justly : for one man's joyous laugh augments earth's joy,
  —is all men's gain.
Scorn not the gift of gladness given to those bright
  souls.   It is from Heaven.

XXVIII.

And, there, are many mansions made : and, here, are
  many ways : and one
Walks safest in the sheltering shade, another in the
  cheering sun.
His sheep the Heavenly Shepherd guides, and pasture fit
  for each provides,

XXIX.

With care for all.   And some His showers shall whiten,
  some His suns shall warm.
Our pains are portion'd to our powers.   His hand may
  hurt, but cannot harm.
But, if the cross be on us laid, and our soul's crown of
  thorns be made,

XXX.

Then, sure, 'twere best to bear the cross; nor lightly
  fling the thorns behind,
Lest we grow happy by the loss of what was noblest in
  the mind.
Here—in the ruins of my years—Master, I thank Thee,
  through these tears !

XXXI.

Thou suffered'st here, and did'st not fail.   Thy bleeding
  feet these paths have trod.
But Thou wert strong, and I am frail : and I am man,
  and Thou art God.
How I have striven, Thou know'st.   Forgive how I
  have fail'd, who saw'st me strive.

XXXII.

It was in the far foreign lands this sickness came upon
  me first.
By hot winds scorching desert sands this fever of the
  south was nurst,
Until it reach'd some vital part.   I die not of a broken
  heart.

XXXIII.

O think not that! If I could live . . . there's much
to live for, worthy life.
It is not for what fame could give—though that I scorn
not—but the strife
Were noble for its own sake too. I thought that I had
much to do—

XXXIV.

But God begins, child, where men end. . . . Hark!
'twas the bittern, as he rose
Against the glaring river-bend. How red your little
casement glows!
The night falls fast. How lonely, dear, this bleak old
house will look next year!

XXXV.

So sad a thought? . . . ah, yes! I know it is not well
to brood on this :
And yet—such thoughts will come and go, unbidden.
'Tis that you should miss,
My darling, one familiar tone of this weak voice when I
am gone.

XXXVI.

Again, that bittern's good-night cry! And what a
melancholy charm
In yonder streak of orange sky! Sweet sister, lend your
gentle arm
To help me back to my old chair. And will you sit
beside me there?

XXXVII.

Such calm is in my soul to-night, and all my life so
    dreamlike seems,
I have no wish to sleep.   For quite awake I dream the
    strangest dreams.
Which you must hear.   Time fleets away.   And still,
    child, still so much to say!

SPRING AND WINTER.

I.

Was it well in him, if he
    Felt not love, to speak of love so?
If he still unmoved must be,
    Was it nobly sought to move so?
—Pluck the flower, but not to wear it—
Spurn it from him, yet not spare it?

II.

Need he say that I was fair,
    With such meaning in his tone,
Adding ever that her hair
    Had the same tinge as my own?
Pluck my life up, root and bloom,
To make garlands for her tomb?

III.

And, her cheek, he said, tho' bright,
    Lack'd the lucid blush divine
Of that rose each whisper light

Of his praises waked in mine;
But 'twas just that he loved then
More than he can love again.

IV.

Then, if beauty could not bind him,
   Wherefore praise me, speaking low ?
Use my face just to remind him
   How no face could please him now ?
Why, if loving could not move him,
Did he teach me still to love him ?

V.

" Yes ! " he said, " he had grown wise now :
   He had suffer'd much of yore :
But a fair face, to his eyes now,
   Was a fair face, and no more.
Yet the anguish and the bliss,
And the dream too, had been his."

VI.

Ah, those words a thought too tender
   For the commonplaces spoken !
Looks whose meaning seem'd to render
   Help to words when speech came broken !
Why so late in July moonlight
Just to say what's said by noonlight ?

VII.

And why praise my youth for gladness,
   Keeping something in his smile
That changed all my youth to sadness,

He still smiling all the while?
Since, when so my youth was over,
He said "seek some younger lover!"

VIII.

Well, the Spring's back now! the thrushes
    Are astir as heretofore,
And the apple blossom blushes
    As of old about the door.
Doth he taste a finer bliss,
I must wonder, in all this,

IX.

(Winning thus what I have lost)
    By the usage of my youth?
—I can feel my forehead crost
    By the wrinkle's fretful tooth,
While the grey grows in my hair,
And the cold creeps everywhere.

SONG FROM "LUCILE."

THE BIRD OF PARADISE.

I.

HEAR a song that was born in the land of my birth!
　The anchors are lifted, the fair ship is free,
And the shout of the mariners floats in its mirth—
　'Twixt the light in the sky and the light on the sea.

II.

And the ship is a world.　She is freighted with souls,
　She is freighted with merchandise; proudly she sails
With the Labour that stores and the Will that controls
　The gold in the ingots, the silk in the bales.

III.

From the gardens of Pleasure, where reddens the rose,
　And the scent of the cedar is faint on the air,
Past the harbours of Traffic, sublimely she goes,
　Man's hopes o'er the world of the waters to bear!

IV.

While the cheer from the harbours of Traffic is heard,
  Where the gardens of Pleasure fade fast on the sight,
O'er the rose, o'er the cedar, there passes a bird,
  'Tis the Paradise Bird, never known to alight.

V.

And that bird, bright and bold as a Poet's desire,
  Roams her own native heavens, the realms of her birth
There she soars like a seraph, she shines like a fire,
  And her plumage has never been sullied by earth.

VI.

And the mariners greet her; there's song on each lip,
  For that bird of good omen, and joy in each eye.
And the ship and the bird and the bird and the ship,
  Together go forth over ocean and sky.

VII.

Fast, fast fades the land! far the rose-gardens flee,
  And far fleet the harbours.   In regions unknown
The ship is alone on a desert of sea,
  And the bird in a desert of sky is alone.

VIII.

In those regions unknown, o'er that desert of air,
  Down that desert of waters—tremendous in wrath,—
The storm-wind Euryclydon leaps from his lair
  And cleaves, through the waves of the ocean, his path.

IX.

And the bird in the cloud, and the ship on the wave,
Overtaken, are beaten about by wild gales ;
And the mariners all rush their cargo to save,
Of the gold in the ingots, the silk in the bales.

X.

Lo ! A wonder which never before hath been heard,
For it never before hath been given to sight;
On the ship hath descended the Paradise Bird,
The Paradise Bird never known to alight !

XI.

The bird which the mariners bless'd, when each lip
Had a song for the omen which gladden'd each eye,
The bright bird for shelter hath flown to the ship
From the wrath on the sea and the wrath in the sky.

XII.

But the mariners heed not the bird any more,
They are felling the masts, they are cutting the sails,
Some are working, some weeping, and some wrangling
o'er
Their gold in the ingots, their silk in the bales.

XIII.

Souls of men are on board; wealth of man in the hold,
And the storm-wind Euryclydon sweeps to his prey;
And who heeds the bird? Save the silk and the gold!
And the bird from her shelter the gust sweeps away !

XIV.

Poor Paradise Bird ! on her lone flight once more,
  Back again in the wake of the wind she is driven -
To be whelm'd in the storm, or above it to soar,
  And, if rescued from ocean, to vanish to heaven !

XV.

And the ship rides the waters and weathers the gales,
  From the haven she nears the rejoicing is heard.
All hands are at work on the ingots, the bales,
  Save a child, sitting lonely, who misses—the Bird !

From "SONGS OF SERVIA."

———

THE STAG AND THE VILA.*

O'ER the mountain, the wild stag browses the mountain
    herbage alone.
At morn he browses, at noon he sickens, at eve he
    maketh moan.
From the rifts of the rocky quarries the Vila hears him
    and calls—
"O beast of the mountain meadows, the woods, and
    the waterfalls,
What sorrow is thine, so great that, browsing at morn,
                  At noon thou ailest?
And now to the stars thou art moaning! What is it
    that thou bewailest?"
And the wild stag answers the Vila, mournfully moaning
    low,—
"O queen of the hills, my sister! I mourn for my lost
    white doe,

---

   * The Vilas are supernatural beings that appear frequently in
the popular poetry of Servia. They are a kind of fierce Oreads
dwelling among the mountains and forests. They are not in-
capable of sympathy with the human race, though their love is
generally treacherous and often fatal.—See *Songs of Servia.*—
NOTE BY AUTHOR.

My milk-white doe, my darling ! from me o'er the moun-
    tain track,
She wander'd away to the fountain; she wander'd and
    never came back.
Either forlornly she wanders, mourning me, missing her
    way,
Or the hunters have follow'd and found her, and she
    hath perish'd—their prey,
Or else she forgets me, the faithless thing ! and ever
    by valley and crag
Strays wanton after a belling note, and follows another
    stag.
If she be lost in the lonesome places, and hollows under
    the moon,
I pray that God of His goodness will guide her back to
    me soon,
But if she follows another stag caring no more to come
    back,
I pray that God in His vengeance guide the hunter fleet
    on her track."

———

LOVE AND SLEEP.

I WALK'D the high and hollow wood, from dawn to
    even-dew,
The wild-eyed wood stared on me and unclasp'd and let
    me thro',
Where mountain pines like great black birds, stood
    percht against the blue.

Not a whisper heaved the woven waof of those warm
    trees;
All the little leaves lay flat, unmoved of bird or breeze;
Day was losing light all round by indolent degrees.

Underneath the brooding branches, all in holy shade,
Unseen hands of mountain things a mossy couch had
    made,
There, asleep, among pale flowers, my beloved was laid.

Slipping down, a sunbeam bathed her brows with
    bounteous gold,
Unmoved upon her maiden breast her heavy hair was
    roll'd,
Her smile was silent as the smile on corpses three hours
    old.

"Oh, God," I thought, "if this be death that makes
    nor sound nor stir !"
My heart stood still with tender awe, I dared not waken
    her,
But to the dear God in the sky, this prayer I did prefer,

"Grant, dear Lord, in the blessèd sky, a warm wind
    from the sea,
To shake a leaf down on my love from yonder leafy tree,
That she may open her sweet eye and haply look on me !"

The dear God from the distant sea a little wind release,
It shook a leaflet from the tree and laid it on her breast,
Her sweet eyes ope'd and look'd on me.   How can I
    tell the rest ?

TITTLE TATTLE.

Two lovers kist in the meadow green;
They thought there was none to espy;
But the meadow green told what it had seen
To the white flock wandering by.
The white flock told it the shepherd,
The shepherd the traveller from far,
The traveller told it the mariner
Watching the pilot star;
The mariner told it his little bark;
The little bark told it the sea ;
The sea told it the river
Flowing down by the lea;
The river told it the maiden's mother,
And so to the maid it came back:
The maiden, as soon as she heard it,
Curst them all for a tell-tale pack.
"Meadow, be barren for ever!
Grass, grow not henceforth from the mould of
      thee !
Flock, be devoured of the wolf!
Shepherd, the Turk seize hold of thee !
Traveller, rot of the fever!
Mariner, drown in the gulf!
Bark, may the whirlwind perplex thee,
And break thee against the shore !
Sea, may the moon ever vex thee !
River, be dry evermore ! "

LOVE CONFERS NOBILITY.

He. VIOLET,* little one mine !
    I would love thee, but thou art so small.
She. Love me, my love, from those heights of thine,
    And I shall grow tall, so tall !
    The pearl is small, but it hangs above
    A royal brow and a kingly mind :
    The quail is little, little, my love,
    But she leaves the hunter behind.

NEGLECTED FLOWERS.

LITTLE violet, drooping all alone, like my own
Drooping heart, I would pluck thee; but there's none,
    no not one,
To whom I dare to give thee ; so I leave thee, and
    pass on.
I would give thee gladly, gladly, if I dared, to Ali Bey ;
But too proud (ah, well-a-day !) is Ali Bey—so they say !
Proud he is ! I do not dare. Would he care, he, to wear
Any flower that buds or blows ?—save the rose, I suppose !

No ! rest there, and despair ! Live or die ! Thou and I
Have no chance to catch one glance from his eye,
    passing by.

  * Violet is a pet name as well as a proper name in Servia.

From "CHRONICLES AND CHARACTERS."

GENSERIC.

GENSERIC, King of the Vandals, who, having laid
    waste seven lands,
From Tripolis far as Tangier, from the sea to the Great
    Desert sands,
Was lord of the Moor and the African,—thirsting anon
    for new slaughter,
Sail'd out of Carthage, and sail'd o'er the Mediterranean
    water;
Plunder'd Palermo, seized Sicily, sack'd the Lucanian
    coast,
And paused, and said, laughing, "Where next?"
            Then there came to the Vandal a Ghost
From the Shadowy Land that lies hid and unknown in
    the Darkness Below.
And answer'd, "To Rome!"
         Said the King to the Ghost, "And whose
    envoy art thou?
Whence comest thou? and name me his name that hath
    sent thee: and say what is thine."
"From far: and His name that hath sent me is God,"
    the Ghost answer'd, "and mine

Was Hannibal once, ere thou wast : and the name that
    I now have is Fate.
But arise, and be swift, and return.   For God waits, and
    the moment is late."
And " I go," said the Vandal.   And went.   When at
    last to the gates he was come,
Loud he knock'd with his fierce iron fist.   And full
    drowsily answer'd him Rome.
" Who is it that knocketh so loud?   Get thee hence.
    Let me be.   For 'tis late."
" Thou art wanted," cried Genseric.   "Open ! His
    name that hath sent me is Fate,
And mine, who knock late, Retribution."
          Rome gave him her glorious things:
The keys she had conquer'd from kingdoms: the crowns
    she had wrested from kings :
And Genseric bore them away into Carthage, avenged
    thus on Rome,
And paused, and said, laughing, " Where next? "
          And again the Ghost answer'd him, " Home !
For now God doth need thee no longer."
        " Where leadest thou me by the hand ? "
Cried the King to the Ghost.   And the Ghost answer'd,
    " Into the Shadowy Land."

THE DAUPHIN.

A PALACE here, a People there,
Face to face, i' the rainy air:
For the rain is raining heavily,
And the sick day shutting a bloodshot eye.

The People, nowhere a while ago,
Now here, now there, now everywhere,
And, of all in the Palace, none doth know
Where the People may be, ere is done
This last of two disastrous days,
Now waning fast, with watery rays.
Quick, Fancy ! ere its light be gone,
From out of the many 'tis darkening on
Save me a single face.   This one.

Broider'd of satin, as best befits,
Is the gilded chair where the urchin sits,
Whose grandsires all earth's greatest were
In grandeur, when the grand were great.
For the childhood of this child is heir
To monarchy's old age.

                The late
Sunbeam, now sinking in his hair
(Weary of strife with a rainy sky)
Faintly, solemnly, lingers there
With a sorrowful glory, soon to die:
As all things must, some day, whene'er
Time disavows them: Time knows why.

O'er kingdoms twain thou wert born to reign,
Bourbon child of the Habsburg mother !
Life's fairest, one: and earth's, the other:
France, and Youth.   Of all the train
Of those the wondering world admires,
Lords and Ladies, Knights and Squires,
Long-robed Senator severe,
Royal Duke, and Princely Peer,
—They whose heads be Heads of France,

To whom, with a sullen countenance,
Hungry hundreds crook the knee,
None but boweth the head to thee,
Little child !   Whose face is one
Of a group that all are gone.

For, since thou, O child, didst flee
(Who knows where?) from human sight,
Never child, kingborn, like thee,
Hath been born to absolute right :
Sons of kings no more can be
Guaranteed, as thou wert then,
Of the servitude of men.

Hearest thou the sounds outside ?
Hearest thou the sounds within ?
In the neighbouring chamber Pride
Stoops, in colloquy with Fear :
Mounier's loyal cares begin :
Prudence plucks at Lafayette :
Orleans with sulky stride
Is philosophising yet :
Chartres hath Louis by the ear :
Necker rubs a ruminant chin.
Outside in the twilight drear
Swells the ominous surly din.

See ! the child is playing now
With his sister's silky tresses :
To whose infantine white brow
Lips as white a mother presses.
Are not children safe from harm,
Circled by a mother's arm ?

In the chair where sits the child
Smiling, long since sat and smiled
Him men named the "Grand Monarque.'
Ah, the light is fading dark !
Thro' the palace windows wide
What is still so dim descried
In the pale persistent rain?

Is the deluge back again?
And what wreckt world's groaning ark
There emits its monstrous train
To new-people earth with pain?
Men or beasts?　What are they?　Mark !
Seest thou?　Hear'st thou, little child?
Haggard faces: women wild :
Men red-handed, blood-defiled :
Heroism, and Hope, and Hate,
Hunger, Horror, Wrath, and Crime,
Mingling in the march of Fate,
Life's grotesque with Love's sublime :
Ragged wretches grim and stark,
Smiling as they never smiled
Till this moment: jaw of shark
Gaping at a drowning ship :
Eye of tiger: lion's grip :
Stormy starvelings, smutcht and soil'd,
Thick thro' garden, court, and park,
Round that palace terrace-piled,
Teeming, tossing, trampling . . . Hark !
First a growl, and then a howl,
Voice of a vast tormented soul,
And then a shrill heart-breaking bark,
And now an immense murtherous roar,
Nearer, drearer, more and more,—
The famisht wild beast's roar for bread !

Suddenly the child's hand ceased
Its sport among the tiny tresses
Of the little golden head
Backward bent to its caresses;
All those tumbled curls released;
While the pouting child-lips said
" MOTHER, I AM HUNGRY ! "

                  Cry
Of the poor man's child, supprest
In a People's starving breast,
For so many wicked years !
Cry, no law could longer smother
In the lawless lifeless past !
By what strange revenge of chance
Didst thou thus ascend so high,
From what depths of woe upcast,
As to smite the heart of a mother,
Heard in the unwilling ears
Of a listening Queen of France,
From a Dauphin's lips at last ?

MISERY.

I.

'TWAS neither day nor night, but both together
Mix'd in a muddy snudge of London weather,
And the dull pouring of perpetual
Dim rain was vague, and vast, and over all.

She stray'd on thro' the mud; 'twas nothing new:
And thro' the rain—the rain? it was mud too!
The woman still was young, and Nature meant,
Doubtless, she should be fair; but'that intent
Hunger, in haste, had marr'd, or toil, or both.
There was no colour in the quiet mouth,
No light in the dim eye. But a wan grace
Of perisht beauty in the thin young face
That lingered ghost-like. There's a last degree
Of misery that is sexless wholly. She
Was woman still, for all her wither'd look,
Even as a faded flower within a book,
Is still a blossom.

       To the bridge she came
Just as the foggy lamps began to flame
Along the loud dark streets. With eyes hard set
She stopp'd there, lean'd against the parapet,
And watch'd the sallow melancholy stream.
The enormous city, like a madman's dream,
Full of strange hummings and unnatural glare,
Beat on her brain. The shadows whisper'd
    " There,
Is quiet, and an end of long distress.
Leap down! leap in! One anguish more or less
God keeps no strict account of." But, to-night,
She still fears those dark whispers. What right
Is hers to die?—a mother, and a wife,
Whose love hath given hostages to life!

The voices of the shadows make reply
" Woman, no right to live is right to die."
Ah no, for Willie waits for her at home,
Ill—then the little ones—no work has come,

Though long she waited, and their rent is due
To-morrow. Ah, to-morrow ! Fiercer grew
The woman's fretful cough. A drunken man
Reel'd past her, stared, and down the dark began
To troll a tavern stave. Up stream'd again
The voices of the shadows, in disdain :

"A mother ? and a wife ? Ill-gotten names,
Filch'd from earth's blisses to increase its shames !
What right have breadless mothers to give birth
To breadless babies?" With the exuberant mirth
Of childhood, three blithe ragged little elves,
Rejoicing in the rain and in themselves,
Ran by her. Then her thoughts began to stray
Far out of London, many a mile away
Among the meadows: in green Hertfordshire
From labyrinthine lanes a grey church spire
Points heavenward, and a hamlet laughs beneath,
Embower'd and haunted by the hawthorn's breath.
"We were so young! we loved each other so!
Ah yet, . . . if one could live the winter thro'!
And winter's worst is o'er in March . . ."
                                        Again
She wander'd onwards, thro' the endless rain
Among the endless streets, with feet slip-shod.
The sky seem'd one vast blackness without God.
The roaring of the wheels began anew,
And London down its dismal vortex drew
This wandering minim of the misery
Of millions.

                    White beneath the filthy sky
And filthy pavement, gleam'd the Workhouse Wall.
She recognised it with thoughts augural
Of worse to come, and shudder'd. 'Twas a thought

Only that made her shudder.   Her foot caught,
However, in a pile of something strange,
And wet, and soft ; which made that shudder change
To one of physical terror.
                              'Twas as tho'
The multitudinous mud, to scare her so,
Had lump'd itself into a hideous heap,
Not human sure, but living.   With a creep
The thing her foot had touch'd began to move,
And from the inward to the outward shove
Layer after layer of soak'd and rotting rags
On each side, down it, to the sloppy flags
Beneath its headless bulk ; thus making space
For the upthrusting of the creature's face,
Or creature's self, whate'er that might have been.
Whence, suddenly emerging, to be seen,
One must imagine, rather than to see,
Since it look'd nowhere, neither seem'd to be
Surprised, nor even conscious, there was thrust
(As tho' it came up thus because it must
And not because it would) a human head,
With sexless countenance, that neither said
To man nor woman . . . " I belong to you,"
But seem'd a fearful mixture of the two.
The woman, only very poor indeed,
Recoil'd before that creature past all need,
And past all help, too, being past all hope.
For, stern and stark, against the solid cope
Of the sad, rainy, and enormous night,
The sexless face had fix'd itself upright
At once, and, as it were, mechanically,
With no surprise ; but seeming to imply
That it had done with this world everywhere,
And only look'd to Heaven ; yet look'd not there
With any sort of hope.

She shrank away
Abasht ; not daring, at the first, to say
Such words as, meant for comfort, might have been
Too much like insult to that grim-faced Queen,
Or King, whiche'er it was, of Wretchedness.
Her own much misery seem'd so much less
Than this. At last, she timidly drew near
And whisper'd faintly in the creature's ear
" Have you no home ? " No look even made reply,
Much less a word. But on the stolid sky
The stolid face stared ever. " Are you cold ? "
A sort of inward creepy movement roll'd
The rain-soak'd lump. And still the stolid face
Perused the stolid sky. Perhaps the case
Supposed was too self-evident to claim
More confirmation than what creeping came
To loosen those wet rags. The woman said
" Are you not hungry ? " Quick the sexless head
Turn'd, and the fingers of a skeleton claw
Rending its foul and tatter'd shroud, you saw
—Was it a woman's breast ?

II.

A sudden shout
Of many voices from the street rang out,
" Stop thief." A man rush'd by these women,—
    rush'd
So vehemently by them, that he brush'd
Their raggedness together,—as he pass'd,
Dropp'd something on the pavement,—and was fast
Wrapp'd in the rainy vapours of the night,
That, in a moment, smear'd him out of sight,
And, in a moment after, let emerge

The trampling crowd; which, all in haste to urge
Its honest chase, swept o'er that wretched twain,
Regardless, and rush'd on into the rain,
Leaving them both, upon the grimy flags,
Bruised, trampled,—rags in colloquy with rags,
And so,—alone.

　　　　　　　　　　Meanwhile the wolfish face,
Resettled to its customary place,
Was staring as before, into the sky,
Stolid.　The other woman heavily
Gather'd herself together, bruised, in pain,
Half rose up, slipp'd on something, and again
Sank feebly back upon her hand.
　　　　　　　　　　　　　　But now
What new emotion shakes her?　Doth she know
What this is, that her clutch upon the stone
Hath felt, and, feeling, closes fiercely on?
This pocket-book? with gold enough within
To feed . . . Alas! and must it be a sin
To keep it?　Were it possible to pay
With what its very robber flings away
For bread . . . bread! . . . bread! . . . and still
　　　not starve, yet still
Be honest!　" Were one doing very ill
If . . . One should pray . . . if one *could* pray, •
　　　that's sure,
The strength would come at last.　We are so poor!
So poor . . . 'tis terrible!　To understand
Such things, one should be learn'd, and have at hand
Ever so many good religious books,
And texts, and things.　And then, one starves.　It
　　　looks
So like a godsend!"　Crouch'd against the wall,

She counted the gold pieces. "Food for all?
Us four and *that* makes five." Again she thought,
Or tried to think, of lessons early taught,
Easy to learn once, in the village school,
When to be honest seem'd the simple rule
For being happy; and of many a text
That task'd old Sundays; growing more perplext,
As, more and more, her giddy memory made
Haphazard catches at the words.

                       " Who said
' Therefore I say unto you ' (ah ! 'twere sweet)
' Have no thought for your lives, what ye shall eat '
(If that were possible !)—' nor what to wear?'
Have no thought (that should mean, then, have no
    care !)
Your Father knoweth of what things ye need
Before ye ask. 'The morrow shall take heed
For its own things !' And still 'tis sure He bade
The people pray, ' Give us our daily bread,'
And elsewhere . . . ' Ask, and ye shall have.'" She
    stopp'd,
And trembled. And the tempting treasure dropp'd
From her faint hand. She snatch'd it up again,
And cried ' Mine ! mine ! be it the Devil's gain
Or God's good gift ! Sure, what folks must, folks may,
And folks must live."

                 She gazed out every way
Along the gloomy street. In desert land
To tempted saints mankind was more at hand
Than now it seem'd to this poor spirit pent
In populous city. Hurriedly, she bent
Above her grim companion, in whose ear
She mutter'd, hoarse and quick . . . " Make haste !
    see here !

Off! off!"   No answer.   To the stolid sky
The stolid face was turn'd immovably.
The sky was dark: the face was dark.   The face
And sky were silent both: you could not trace
The faintest gleam of light in the dark look
Of either.   Vehemently the woman shook
That miserable mass of rags.   It let
Itself be shaken: did not strive to get
Up, or away: said nought.   A worried rat
So lets itself be shaken by a cat
Or mastiff, when the vermin's back, 'tis clear,
Is snapp'd, and there's no more to feel, or fear.
"Oh haste!"   No answer.   "It is late, late
       Come!"
No answer.   Those lean jaws were lock'd and
       dumb.
Then o'er the *living* woman's face there spread
Death's hue reflected.
                    "Late! . . . too late!" she said.
"O Heaven, to die *thus!*"   With a broken wail
She turn'd, and fled fast, fast.   Fled whither?

                         III.

                                        Pale
Thro' the thick vagueness of the vaporous night,
From the dark alley, with a clouded light,
Two rheumy, melancholy lampions flare.
They are the eyes of the Police.
                              In there,
Down the dark archway, thro' the greasy door,
Passionately pushing past the three or four
Complacent constables that cluster'd round
A costermonger, in the gutter found
Incapably, but combatively, drunk,

The woman hurried. Thro' the doorway slunk
A peaky pinch'd-up child with frighten'd face,
Important witness in some murder case
About to come before the magistrate
To-morrow. At a dingy table sat
The slim Inspector, spectacled, severe,
Rapidly writing. In a sort of fear
Of seeing it again, she shut her eyes
And flung it down there. With sedate surprise
The man look'd up. "Because I do not know
The owner, sir" . . . she said. "A while ago
I found it. And there's money in it . . . much,
Oh, so much money, sir!" A hungry touch
Of the defeated Tempter made her wince
To see him count it. Such a short while since
She, too, had done the same.

             "Your name? address?"
She gave them. Easy, from the last, to guess
Their wretchedness who dwelt in such a place!
The shrewd and practised eye perused her face
Contented, not surprised; for they that see
Crime oftenest, oftenest, too, see honesty
Where most of us would seldom look for it,
Or find it with surprise . . . in rags, to wit.

"Honest and poor. Deserves a large reward.
No doubt there'll be one." "Ah, the times are hard,
So hard, God help us all! and, sir, indeed
We are so poor. Two little mouths to feed.
If one could only get some work to do!"
"Ah . . . married? out of work? and children?
     two?
Mem. Let the owner know, if found. Good night."
But still she stood there. He had turn'd to write.

She stood, and eyed him with a dreary eye,
And did not move.   He look'd up presently.
"Not gone yet? eh? what more?"   "And, sir,"
. . . she said,
"There's by the Workhouse wall a woman . . .
dead.
There was no room within, sir, I suppose.
There are so many of them.   Heaven knows
'Tis hard for such as we to understand
How such things happen in a Christian land."

Her face twitch'd, and her cough grew fierce again,
As she pass'd out into the night and rain.

THE APPLE OF LIFE.

FROM the river Euphrates, the river whose source is in
Paradise, far
As red Egypt,—sole lord of the land and the sea, 'twixt
the eremite star
Of the orient desert's lone dawn, and the porch of the
chambers of rest
Where the great sea is girded with fire, and Orion returns
in the west,
As the ships come and go in grand silence,—King
Solomon reign'd.   And behold,
In that time there was everywhere silver as common as
stones be, and gold
That for plenty was 'counted as silver, and cedar as
sycamore trees

That are found in the vale, for abundance. For GOD to
    the King gave all these,
With glory exceeding; moreover all kings of the earth to
    him came,
Because of his wisdom, to hear him. So great was King
    Solomon's fame.
And, for all this, the King's soul was sad. And his
    heart said within him, " Alas,
For man dies ! if his glory abideth, himself from his
    glory shall pass.
I have planted me gardens and vineyards, and gotten me
    silver and gold,
And my hand from whatever my heart hath desirèd I did
    not withhold :
And what profit have I in the works of my hand which I
    take not away ?
I have searchèd out wisdom and knowledge: and what
    do they profit me, they?
As the fool dieth, so doth the wise. What is gather'd is
    scatter'd again.
As the breath of the beasts, even so is the breath of the
    children of men:
And the same thing befalleth them both. And not any
    man's soul is his own."

    This he thought as he sat in his garden, and watch'd
    the great sun going down.
And " Behold," said the King, " in a moment the
    glory shall vanish ! " Even then,
While he spake he was 'ware of a man drawing near him,
    who seem'd to his ken
(By the hair in its blackness like flax that is burn'd in the
    hemp-dresser's shed,
And the brow's smoky hue, and the smouldering eyeball
    more livid than lead)

As the sons of the land that lies under the sword of the
    Cherub whose wing
Wraps in wrath the shut gateways of Paradise. He,
    being come to the King,
Seven times made obeisance before him. To whom,
    "What art thou," the King cried,
"That thus unannounced to King Solomon comest?"
    The man, spreading wide
The palm of his right hand, show'd in it an apple yet
    bright from the Tree
In whose stem springs the life never-failing that Sin lost
    to Adam, when he,
Tasting knowledge forbidden, found death in the fruit of
    it. . . So doth the Giver
Evil gifts to the evil apportion. And "Hail! let the
    King live for ever!"
Bowing down at the feet of the monarch, and laughingly,
    even as one
Whose meaning, in joy or in jest, hovers hid 'twixt the
    word and the tone,
Said the stranger (as lightly the apple he laid in the hand
    of the King),
"From between the four rivers of Eden, Jehovah hath
    sent me, to bring
To his servant King Solomon, even to my lord that on
    Israel's throne
He hath 'stablisht, this fruit from the Tree in whose
    branch Life abideth: for none
That hath tasted this apple shall die." Then he
    vanish'd. The monarch perused
The strange fruit that, alluring his lip, in his hand lay
    untasted. He mused—
"Life is good: but not life for life's sake. Life eternal,
    eternally young,

That, indeed, were a life to be prized; when the jubilant
    spirit is strong,
When in veins unfatigued the still bountiful pulses of
    happiness beat,
And the dews of the dawn of Desire on the roses of
    Beauty are sweet!
But what gain were in living forever, when life is unfit
    to engage
The sad care it yet craves? Life eternal, eternally
    wedded to Age?
When the hand saith '*I did,*' not '*I will do,*' the
    heart saith '*It was,*' not "*'Twill be,*'
Then too late is the gift of Forever, and too late comes
    this apple to me."
He arose. And wherever the sunlight had been, there
    was moonlight, and deep
In their odorous shadows the myrtle and rose were
    already asleep.
As, with difficult steps, he went feebly, by garden and
    terrace and court,
On his sceptre he lean'd; for that sceptre to him was a
    staff for support,
Tho' to others a rod of dominion. And so to his House
    he return'd.
There, in ivory chambers sweet lamps, that were
    scented with cinnamon, burn'd,
And innumerous columns, 'twixt curtains of crimson,
    stood gather'd in groves
Thick as trees of the forest in Libanus stand, where the
    wind, as it moves,
Whispers, "I, too, am Solomon's servant!"—huge
    trunks hid in garlands of gold,
On whose tops the skill'd sculptors of Sidon had granted
    men's gaze to behold

How the phœnix that sits on the cedar's lone summit
    'mid fragrance and fire,
Ever dying and living, hath loaded with splendours her
    funeral pyre;
How the stork builds her nest on the pine-top; the date
    from the palm-branch depends;
And the shaft of the blossoming aloe soars crowning the
    life which it ends.
And, from hall on to hall pacing slowly, the King mused
    . . . "O fair Shulamite!
Thy beauty is brighter than starlight on Hebron when
    Hebron is bright,
Thy sweetness is sweeter than Carmel. The King rules
    the nations; but thou,
Thou rulest the King, my Belovèd."

            So murmur'd King Solomon low
To himself, as he pass'd thro' the portal of porphyry,
    that dripp'd, as he pass'd,
From the myrrh-sprinkled wreaths on the locks and the
    lintels; and enter'd at last,
Still sighing, the sweet cedarn chamber, contrived for
    repose and delight,
Where the beautiful Shulamite slumber'd. And straight-
    way, to left and to right,
Bowing down as he enter'd, the Spirits in bondage to
    Solomon, there
Keeping watch o'er his love, sank their swords, spread
    their wings, and evanish'd in air.
The King with a kiss woke the sleeper. And, showing
    the fruit in his hand,
"Behold! this was brought me erewhile by one coming,"
    he said, "from the land
That lies under the sword of the Cherub 'twas pluckt by
    strange hands from the tree

Of whose fruit whoso tasteth shall die not. And there-
    fore I give it to thee,
Best beloved of the daughters of women! The garment,
    tho' broider'd with gold,
Wears away as the moth feeds upon it. So I, in my
    glory, grow old.
But all thine, at the best and the brightest, thou Spirit
    of Beauty and Bliss,
Are the grace and the gladness of youth. Wherefore
    thine, and thine only, be this!
Keep the gift I resign, never losing the freshness and
    sweetness of life,
And of women forever the fairest shall still be King
    Solomon's wife!"
And he dropp'd in her bosom the apple.

        But wistfully, when he was gone,
And the beautiful Shulamite, eyeing the gift of the King,
    sat alone,
"Youth and beauty," she mused, "are but gifts to be
    prized for the love they inspire,
And forever to love and be loved—that, no doubt, were a
    life to desire.
But I love neither beauty nor youth if unloved by my
    loved one they be,
For in life is no loveliness save to be loved, Azariah, by
    thee!"
Then she summon'd, to veil her, the Spirits in bondage
    to Solomon's ring
(For that talisman dread, for a toy, had been given to
    her by the King),
And her form from the vision of mortals they veil'd.
    Thro' the streets, unespied,
She went forth to the door of the house of the Prince
    Azariah, and cried

"It is I ! Dost thou hear my heart beating?   Thy love
 is more comely than gold,
And more precious to me is thy kiss than a life that can
 never grow old !"
Azariah arose, and unbolted the door to the fair
 Shulamite.
"O my queen, what dear folly is this?   For as spies are
 the stars of the night,
And at that which is done in the chamber the leak in the
 housetop shall peep,
And the hand of a king smiteth hard, and the eyes of a
 king never sleep!"
But the beautiful Shulamite answer'd, "Nay, fear not,
 for lo, what I bring!
'Tis the fruit of the tree that in Eden Jehovah hides under
 the wing
Of the Cherub that chased away Adam.   And who of
 this apple doth taste,
He shall live and not die.   Wherefore fear thou not
 death! for the gift that in haste
I have brought thee is life everlasting."   But soon as the
 Prince was alone
With her gift, as he lean'd from the lattice he mutter'd,
 " 'Tis well! she is gone ! "
From his lattice he heard down the streets of the city the
 tripping of feet
And the voices of youths running after.   And "*Life,*"
 sang a wanton, " *is sweet*
Long as lasts the good minute."   " Not long," sigh'd the
 Prince, " doth the good minute last !
What of life, when it goes?"   Then he caught up the
 apple, and forth with it pass'd
To the house of the harlot Egyptian, and mused as he
 went—" Life is good

Just so long as the joy of it lasts, while a man doeth that
    which he would,
Goeth whither he listeth, and pleaseth himself be the
    chance what it may.
Shall I care to be loved by a queen, if her love with my
    freedom I pay?
No, the *May-be* for me, not the *Must-be!* The field where
    the wild blossom springs,
Not the rose that is guarded by dragons to brighten the
    precincts of kings!
Open, open, thou dark-eyed beguiler of darkness!"

            Uprose to his knock,
Light of foot, the lascivious Egyptian, and lifted the
    latch from the lock,
And open'd, and led in the prince to her chamber, and
    pour'd him the wine
Wherewith she first brighten'd the moist lips that mur-
    mur'd, "Ha, fool! Art thou mine?
I am thine. This will last for an hour." And then,
    humming strange words from a song
Sung by maidens in Memphis the old, when they bore
    the Crown'd Image along,
She sprang loose from his clasp, and danced round him.
    "Say, fool. What good gift dost thou bring?"
Azariah toss'd to her the apple, and answer'd, "A gift
    for a king!"
"Go to, it is nought, fool! An apple." "But an
    apple that comes from the Tree
Of whose fruit whoso tastes lives for ever. I care not.
    I give it to thee.
Nay, witch! 'tis worth more than the shekels of gold
    thou hast charm'd from my purse.
Take it. Eat. Life is sweeter than knowledge: and
    Eve, thy sly mother, fared worse."

" Fool, why dost thou laugh?" and he answer'd,
   " Because, witch, it tickles my brain
Intensely to think that all we, that be Something while
   yet we remain,
We, the princes of people—ay, even the King's self—
   shall die in our day,
And thou, that art Nothing, shall sit on our graves, with
   our grandsons, and play."
But anon, when alone, with the fruit in her hand still
   untasted, perusing
Her mysterious prize, the dark woman, perplext by sad
   doubts, fell a musing,
And she thought. . . . " What is Life without Honour?
   And what can the life that I live
Give to me, I shall care to continue, not caring for aught
   it can give?
I? The man call'd me Nothing. He said well. The
   great in their glory must go,
And shall I go on living forever a life that is shameful
   and low?"
Her tears fell. They fell on the apple. " 'Tis a gift for
   a king," did he say?
Ay, a king's life is life as it should be—a life like the
   light of the day
Wherein all that liveth rejoiceth. For whom then this
   gift? Not for me,
Nor the fool Azariah that sold it for folly. The King!
   only he,—
Only he hath the life that's worth living for ever.
   Whose life, not alone
Is the life of the King, but the life of the many made
   mighty in one.
To the King will I carry this apple. And he (for the
   hand of a king

Is a fountain of hope) in his handmaid shall honour the
    gift that I bring.
And men for this deed shall esteem me, with Rahab by
    Israel praised,
As first among those who, tho' lowly, their shame into
    honour have raised."
So she rose, and went forth thro' the city. And with
    her the apple she bore
In her bosom: and stood 'mid the multitude, waiting
    therewith in the door
Of the hall where the King, to give judgment, ascended
    at morning his throne:
And, kneeling there, cried, " Let the King live for ever!
    Behold, I am one
Whom the vile of themselves count the vilest. But
    great is the grace of my lord.
And now let my lord on his handmaid look down, and
    give ear to her word.
For on me was this apple bestow'd, that thy servant
    should eat and not die.
But I said to the soul of thy servant, ' Not so. For
    behold, what am I,
That the King, in his glory and gladness, should cease
    from the light of the sun,
Whilst I, that am least of his slaves, in my shame and
    abasement live on?'
For not sweet is the life of thy servant, unless to thy
    servant, my lord
Stretch his hand, and show favour. For surely the frown
    of a king is a sword,
But the smile of the king is as honey that flows from the
    clefts of the rock,
And his grace is as dew that from Horeb descends on the
    heads of the flock:

As the grapes of the vines of En-Gedi are favours that
    fall from his hands,
And as towers on the hill-tops of Shenir the throne of
    King Solomon stands.
But how shall one lose what he hath not? Who hath,
    let him keep what he hath.
Wherefore I to the King give this apple."

       Then great was King Solomon's wrath,
And he rose, rent her garment, and cried, "Woman,
    whence came this apple to thee?"
But when he was 'ware of the truth, then his heart was
    awaked, and said he,
"From the Angel of Death came the gift. Life rejects
    it. Jehovah is just.
Let man's spirit to Him whence it cometh return, and his
    dust to the dust!"

––––––––

LAST WORDS.

OF A SENSITIVE SECOND-RATE POET.

WILL, are you sitting and watching there yet? And I
    know, by a certain skill
That grows out of utter wakefulness, the night must be
    far spent, Will:
For, lying awake so many a night, I have learn'd at last
    to catch
From the crowing cock, and the clanging clock, and the
    sound of the beating watch,
A misty sense of the measureless march of Time, as he
    passes here,

Leaving my life behind him; and I know that the dawn
    is near.
But you have been watching three nights, Will, and you
    look'd so wan to-night,
I thought, as I saw you sitting there, in the sad mono-
    tonous light
Of the moody night-lamp near you, that I could not
    choose but close
My lids as fast, and lie as still, as tho' I lay in a doze:
For, I mused, " He will think I am dreaming, and then
    he may steal away,
And sleep a little: and this will be well." And truly, I
    dream'd, as I lay
Wide awake, but all as quiet, as tho', the last office done,
They had streak'd me out for the grave, Will, to which
    they will bear me anon.
Dream'd; for old things and places came dancing about
    my brain,
Like ghosts that dance in an empty house: and my
    thoughts went slipping again
By green back-ways forgotten to a stiller circle of time,
Where violets, faded for ever, seem'd blowing as once in
    their prime:
And I fancied that you and I, Will, were boys again as
    of old,
At dawn on the hill-top together, at eve in the field by
    the fold;
Till the thought of this was growing too wildly sweet to
    be borne,
And I oped mine eyes, and turn'd me round, and there,
    in the light forlorn,
I find you sitting beside me. But the dawn is at hand, I
    know.
Sleep a little. I shall not die to-night. You may leave
    me. Go.

Eh! is it time for the drink? must you mix it? it does
    me no good.
But thanks, old friend, true friend! I would live for your
    sake, if I could.
Ay, there are some good things in life, that fall not away
    with the rest.
And, of all best things upon earth, I hold that a faithful
    friend is the best.
For woman, Will, is a thorny flower: it breaks, and we
    bleed and smart:
The blossom falls at the fairest, and the thorn runs into
    the heart.
And woman's love is a bitter fruit; and, however he bite
    it, or sip,
There's many a man has lived to curse the taste of that
    fruit on his lip.
But never was any man yet, as I ween, be he whosoever
    he may,
That has known what a true friend is, Will, and wish'd
    that knowledge away.
You were proud of my promise, faithful despite of my
    fall,
Sad when the world seem'd over-sweet, sweet when the
    world turn'd gall.

O woman-eyes that have smiled and smiled, O woman-
    lips that have kist
The life-blood out of my heart, why thus for ever do you
    persist,
Pressing out of the dark all round, to bewilder my dying
    hours
With your ghostly sorceries brew'd from the breath of
    your poison-flowers?
Still, tho' the idol be broken, I see at their ancient revels,

The riven altar around, come dancing the selfsame devils.
Lente currite, lente currite, noctis equi!
Linger a little, O Time, and let me be saved ere I die!
How many a night 'neath her window have I walk'd in
the wind and rain,
Only to look at her shadow fleet over the lighted pane!
Alas! 'twas the shadow that rested, 'twas herself that
fleeted, you see,
And now I am dying, I know it:—dying, and where is
she?
Dancing divinely, perchance, or, over her soft harp
strings,
Using the past to give pathos to the little new song that
she sings.
Bitter? I dare not be bitter in the few last hours left to
live.
Needing so much forgiveness, God grant me at least to
forgive.
Not to know vice is virtue, not fate, however men rave:
And, next to this I hold that man to be but a coward and
slave
Who bears the plague-spot about him, and, knowing it,
shrinks or fears
To brand it out, tho' the burning knife should hiss in his
heart's hot tears.
Yet oh! the confident spirit once mine, to dare and to
do!
Take the world into my hand, and shape it, and make it
anew:
Gather all men in my purpose, men in their darkness and
dearth,
Men in their meanness and misery, made of the dust of
the earth,
Mould them afresh, and make out of them Man, with his
spirit sublime,

Man, the great heir of Eternity, dragging the conquests
    of Time!
Therefore I mingled among them, deeming the poet
    should hold
All natures saved in his own, as the world in the ark
    was, of old.

Triple fool in my folly! purblind and impotent worm,
Thinking to move the world, who could not myself stand
    firm!
Cheat of a worn-out trick, as one that on shipboard roves
Wherever the wind may blow, still deeming the con-
    tinent moves.
Friend, lay your hand in my own, and swear to me,
    when you have seen
My body borne out from the door, ere the grass on my
    grave shall be green,
You will burn every book I have written.   And so
    perish, one and all,
Each trace of the struggle that fail'd with the life that I
    cannot recall.
Where was the fault?   Was it strength fell short!   And
    yet (I can speak of it now)
How my spirit sang like the resonant nerve of a warrior's
    battle bow
When the shaft has leapt from the string, what time, her
    first bright banner unfurl'd,
Song aim'd her arrowy purpose in me sharp at the heart
    of the world!
Comfort me not.   For if aught be worse than failure
    from over-stress
Of a life's prime purpose, it is to sit down content with a
    little success.
Talk not of genius baffled.   Genius is master of man.

Genius does what it must, and Talent does what it can.
And pity me not.   For death to me is a boon far better
  than fame.
It is only ceasing to die, Will, of a life that has miss'd
  its aim.
From another life, in another world, new aims must arise.
  And there
New efforts' sweetest reward may be the redemption of
  failure here.

From "ORVAL."

—

EPITHALAMIUM.

ERE the moon is washt down by the wave in the west
    (O thought dread and sweet !),
Ere the nightingale, roused by the moon, is at rest,
    They shall meet !
They, the twain, who were taught by the prescient
    Power
That gave sweets to the bee, giving scents to the flower,
    To find in each other, what few find out,
      The one thing sweet in a world so sour,
      The one thing sure in a life of doubt !
        They shall meet, oh, where ?
        They the Strong and the Fair,
In what hour, not of time, in what land, not of earth ?
Where to breathe is to kindle, and being is birth,
Where the soul and the sense are one feeling alone,
As the heaven and the moonlight are two and yet one ;
      When the eyes from the lips
        Drink delicious eclipse,
      While, in rose-braided car,
        Love, free lord of his own,
      To the fair, the afar,

The unseen, the unknown,
Thro' faint depths of dim fire
Is drawn, with tugg'd rein,
By the steeds of Desire,
In strong triumph amain,
'Twixt the twilit courts of the orient porch
Of the Dawn of Life ; where the bashful train
Of those tender, timorous Spirits, that are
The bearers bright of his blushing torch,
Are waiting the will of the Morning Star,
To unfasten the portals the Destinies bar
On the brave, bold world, that is yet unborn,
Of the resolute race that is yet to be,
When the sunrise of Freedom, in Truth's fair morn,
Shall be solemn and bright over land and sea,
And all earth be one nation, whose name is borne,
Trampling tyranny, scorning scorn,
By the gentle, the just, and the free !

From " *MISCELLANEOUS POEMS.*"

———

ODE TO A STARLING.

Spring's pilot, and her nimblest-wingèd darling,
  Despite the arrowy-flighted Swallow
  That in thy wake doth follow,
To rob thee of renown, intrepid Starling !
  Full weary of old Winter, sick of sorrow,
As I lay a-drowsing in the dark at dawn of day,
  Seeking to shut from sight a sunless morrow,
And suing to assist me flitting Sleep, that would not
      stay,
    Out of dim lands remote
    Came a hoarse but happy note ;
And then a scatter'd rustling loud beyond the lattice
      eaves
Of jostled wings, a-riot in the rare and rainy leaves.
    Surely, surely, saucy angel
    Of the Virgin Spring's evangel,
    'Twas the sound of thee and thine
    Singing songs yet somewhat hoarser
      For the sea-wind and the brine
    Breathed and braved by each precursor
      Of May's azure and sunshine.

I, at least, thy voice believing,
  And, in responsive mood,
Religiously receiving
  Its prophecies of good,
All the morn long have been roaming
  The wet field and wintry wood,
The burthen of an old song humming :—
" The starlings are come ! and merry May,
And June, and the white thorn, and the hay,
And the violet, and then the rose, and all sweet things
      are coming ! "
    But O ill-welcom'd bird !
      Thy most impassion'd lays
    By heedless ears are heard.
Thou comest before thy time, and unattended.
      The sluggard Spring delays
        To justify thy word ;
      And rancorous Winter stays
To wreak on thee the wrath of frosts and rains offended ;
      Whilst thou of sunny days
        Still singest, undeterr'd
      By scorn or stinted praise,
Befriending thus a land that leaves thee unbefriended.
Envy not thou Cëyx, or Halcyon,
  Their sultry seas, fair-meadow'd lands of fable,
And foamless isles, the tempest strikes not on,
  That sleep in harbours green and hospitable ;
For thou, within thyself, despite foul weather,
  Hast golden calms and glories
Like windless lights where wizards meet together
  On stormy promontories.
Leave to the soft luxurious Nightingale
  Her amorous revels and embower'd delights
Where, over lush rose leaves the balmy gale
  Is breathing low thro' blue midsummer nights.

Thine is the bardic chant, the battle strain,
   The strenuous impulse thine,
Antagonising wind and sleety rain
   In the tough-headed pine.
Leave to the Lark his lucid chariotings
   And mirth Memnonian, when auroral skies
With shining azure bathe his lyric wings.
   Thy realm beyond to-morrow's orient lies,
Safe from the reach of this anarchic time,
   Where unreveal'd primroses,
And many a lurking love, and budding rhyme
   Each note of thine discloses.
        Thy friends are yet unborn:
          The earliest violet,
        The first bud on the thorn,
          The first wan cowslip, wet
        With tears of the first morn
          That doth such joys beget.
        Thy foes are yet a-dying ;
          Ragged-skirted rains,
        Winds at random flying
          Fast with cloudy manes,
        And the last snows, lying
          Lost on chilly plains.
        Grief and Joy together
          Colloquise with thee :
        Sad and sunny weather
          Shift around the tree
        Where, not heeding either,
          Thou dost carol free
      A music over-winging
    On laughter-lifted pinions
  Earth's bleakness and despair,
      Like old Amphion's singing,
    To raise serene dominions

And fashion from void air,
  Stirr'd by the nimbly-sounding minions
Of its mysterious mandate, everywhere
  Those blossomy battlements,
  And florid tents,
Where, in due time, shall dwell
  All the delicious sights, and sounds, and scents
Of Spring's green citadel.

THE LAY OF THE COCK.

I.

WHO will awaken the Lay of the Cock?
Who will praise his prowess and power?
Who will sing of his virtues seven?

II.

If there be any of mortal stock
Worthy to say " I will waken that lay,"
Uplifted high on a lofty tower
Where the light is holy and fresh from heaven,
In a white robe stoled, with a harp of gold,
Loud, in the hearing of gods and men,
Let him smite his harp at the matin hour
To a note like jubilant Memnon's, when
That strong marmorean mouth of his
From the rapturous east a reorient ray
Of his mother's fairest effulgences
Did, with a mystical fiery touch,
To a sudden ethereal melody wake.

Alas, that in me is no music such
As would then be heard for my hero's sake!
But albeit unfit, magnanimous bird,
Thy bard to be, since slumbering still
Are the worthier singers, here, undeterr'd
By mine own unworth, and my want of skill,
I make essay, at the dawn of day,
In honour of thine to awaken the lay,
And, as tho' I stood on a lofty tower
Where the light is holy and fresh from heaven,
In a white robe stoled, with a harp of gold,
To hymn high praise of thy prowess and power,
And do homage in song to thy virtues seven.

III.

Handmaid of heroes, Martial Muse!
Bring me hither a burnisht shield,
Broad as the targe of Idomeneus *
When forth he strode to the battlefield!
By the mighty spirits of warriors old
Let the orb of that mighty shield be borne:
And roll me hither, thro' heavens that hold
High pageant aglow with the triumphing Morn,
Aurora's chariots, whose chargers bold
The youngest-born of the Hours adorn
With housing of glory and harness of gold!
Then, ere the ardours of sunrise faint,
Or ever a gorgeous cloud grow wan,
Dip me the pencil in each bright dye
Of that dazzling pomp, that I may paint
Whom but the hero that marcheth by
In robes of honour regalian,

* A cock was painted on the shield of Idomeneus.

Mail'd and mantled, with crest on high,
The valorous marshal of Day's blithe van.

IV.

And all the while, by down and dale
Where dews are fresh and light is clear,
From far away i' the buxom gale
Let brave-mouth'd bronzen music come
Of chiding trump and thunderous drum,
Thrilling the heart of the man who may hear,
Like the moving on of some marvellous tale
Of chivalry, joust, and knightly cheer.

V.

With royal train, whose sheeny stain
Is sable shot with emerolde;
Breastplate broad of brightest gold;
Scarlet crest, thick turreted
As Cybele's, on stately head;
Beard of ruddier tinct than is
(If old legends lie not) his
Who, full-arm'd, is slumbering still
Hid in the heart of Salzburg hill;
Shining cuishes, greaves of steel;
Spleenful spur on knightly heel;
Who is he doth lightly leap,
Flashing forth o' the night's dim tent
When the dew is deep, and the lark asleep,
Orient arms in the Orient?

VI.

It is the guardian, gallant and gay,
Of the great world's drowsy conscience. Day

By day he doth in the twilight wan
Rise up, and, with resonant roundelay,
From the cloven caverns of dream unlock
Sleep's bondsmen, speeding upon their way
The wills and wishes of waken'd man.
How shall we hail him? what is his name?
His names are many, for wide his fame;
Blue-helm'd Bellona's champion,
The Bird of Mars, Alectryon,
The Bird of Fire, the Bird of Lok;
Sacred sire of a sacred clan;
Faithfullest chief of the feathery flock
Since temples arose in Asia,
Or priests and augurs their rites began,
Roman, Grecian, Arabian,
And Runic,—they whose spells could sway
Sea-hurricanes Scandinavian.

VII.

Wise and wary as one should be
That is vigilant lord of the virtues seven,
First of all upon earth is he
To watch, and be ware of, change in heaven.
For in heaven a bride he hath; and she
Is starry, tender, and fair to see;
Whose mystical name is Alcyon.*
To her he merrily three times three
Soundeth his strepitant clarion.
Since nothing hath he to hide; but, free
And open, he beareth wherever he wend
A fearless front and a spirit bold
In all his wooings and all his wars.

* The constellation of the Pleiades was called by the Arabian
astronomers "The Hen and Chickens."

Which well they knew, those Flamens old
Who in honour did hold for his corselet of gold,
His stately stride, and his crest on end,
The armèd comrade of mighty Mars,
And fair Minerva's familiar friend.

VIII.

When he walketh under the vaulted arch
Wherethro' a mounted knight might march
At easy speed his pacing steed
Nor bruise one plume of his helmet crest,
This bird, whose magnanimous graciousnesses
The least of his kingly gestes expresses,
Hath so lofty a heart in so lordly a breast
That, with condescensive and sidelong tread,
Lightly he boweth his stately head,
For courtesy's sake, as becometh a king
With his vassals around him progressing.

IX.

Then up on a great sunbeam he springeth,
His clashing vans doth thrice unlock
With a shudder of joy, and make sweet shock
Of all his silken sheeny feathers;
And wingeth, but not far he wingeth,
His weighty flight, erect and tall
Descending on the breezy wall,
Where he with voice sonorous singeth,
After the fashion of his forefathers
To rally his clan from far away,
His ancient famous roundelay.
But first, as when in martial Rome,

Before the Conscript Fathers all,
Uprising with importance, some
Famed leader senatorial
Assumed imposing attitude,
With gather'd robe and right arm bare,
So he, in oratoric mood,
With finger'd foot upcurl'd in air,
Fit posture doth select; then high
And shrill is heard the rallying cry
Whereto, his kinsmen, answering him
From distant regions, make reply;
While he, with inward ecstasy,
Doth either dim blue eyelid film
Let fall o'er each delighted eye.

X.

Anon, the noon is high up-wheel'd,
And reapers droop in oaten field.
But he for whom my harp I string
(So might I half his glory share!)
In easy state, an orient king,
Gracious, grave, and debonair,
Thro' his throng'd seraglio moveth
'Mid his strutting queens; and, stately,
One he seeketh, one reproveth,
Ruling all sedately.
Well-skill'd in government is he,
High-couraged, honourable,
And gentle-manner'd, as should be
Good kings whose thrones are stable:
Wise, loving, watchful as a star,
By lofty thoughts uplifted;
And, birds or men, full few there are
So affluently gifted.

XI.

Chanted and told to a harp of gold,
Upon seven strings, should his virtues be;
That be sevenfold as, in time of old,
Were the Seven Spirits of Chivalrie:
Noble Valour, that feareth none:
Prudence, that keepeth what Valour hath won:
Vigilance wary, and Courtesy kind :
Love, that gives life to all virtues combined:
Justice, that fails not, whatever befall:
And Temperance, setting the measure to all.
Chanted and told to a harp of pure gold,
Upon strings that are seven, with song sevenfold,
Worthy to be are his virtues.   And we,
If we were as bold, as loving, as free,
High-hearted, strong-soul'd, and wise, as he,
As sober, vigorous, vigilant, just,
And joyous, and scornful of mean mistrust,
Then the world would be what the world to me
Doth seem when I hear, in the sunshine clear,
This minstrel making magnanimous cheer,
And hailing the light with a heart of glee.
For his brave song teacheth timely content:
And, far as it reacheth, my soul is sent,
Honouring God's good government,
And greeting the general joy of the world:
While music without, and mirth within,
Mingle my heart with the merry din
Of a loud and high defiance hurl'd
At darkness, and sorrow, and sin.

LITTLE ELLA.

I.

I KNOW now, little Ella, what the flowers
  Said to you then, to make your cheek so pale;
And why the blackbird in our laurel bowers
  Spake to you only, and the timorous snail
Fear'd less your steps than those of the May shower.
  It is not strange these creatures loved you so,
  And told you all. 'Twas not so long ago
You were yourself a bird, or else a flower.

II.

And, little Ella, you were pale because
  So soon you were to die. I know that now.
And why there ever seem'd a sort of gauze
  Over your deep blue eyes, and sad young brow.
You were too good to grow up, Ella, you,
  And be a woman, such as I have known!
  And so upon your heart they put a stone,
And left you, child, among the flowers and dew.

III.

O thou, the morning star of my sad soul!
  My little elfin friend from Faëry Land!
Whose memory is yet innocent of the whole
  Of that which makes me doubly need thy hand,
Thy guiding hand from mine so soon withdrawn!
  Here, where I find so little like to thee,
  For thou wert as the breath of dawn to me,
Starry, and pure, and brief, as is the dawn.

IV.

Thy knight was I, and thou my Faëry Queen.
('Twas in the days of love and chivalry!)
And thou did'st hide thee in a bower of green.
But thou so well hast hidden thee, that I
Have never found thee since. And thou did'st set
  Many a task, and quest, and high emprize,
  Ere I should win from thine approving eyes
My guerdon,—ah! so many, that not yet

V.

My tasks are ended, nor my wanderings o'er.
  But some day there will come across the main
A magic barque, and I shall quit this shore
  Of care, and find thee in thy bower again;
And thou wilt say, "My brother, hast thou found
  Our home at last?" . . . Whilst I, in answer,
    sweet,
  Shall heap my life's last booty at thy feet,
And bare my breast with many a bleeding wound.

VI.

The spoils of time! the trophies of a world!
  The keys of conquer'd towns, and captived kings,
And many a broken sword, and banner furl'd,
  The heads of giants, and swart soldan's rings,
And many a maiden's scarf, and many a wand
  Of baffled wizard, many an amulet,
  And many a shield with mine own heart's blood
    wet,
And jewels rare from many a distant land!

717

VII.

How sweet with thee, my sister, to renew
    The happy search for those ethereal birds
Which back to their own climes thou did'st pursue,—
    Ah, heedless! thou, in all whose deeds and words
Unkindness never was till then, nor lack
    Of care for others' pain! Could'st thou but see
    How woeful weary is my want of thee,
Methinks that even now thou would'st come back;

VIII.

Leaving thy heavenly playmates, for my sake,
    To let me lean my head upon thy breast,
And weep away those worst of griefs that ache
    And scorch, but cannot turn to tears. Or, best,
The way that leads where thou art gone, contrive,
    O child, to whisper to me! Ope the gate,
    And help me thro'. Else, I shall die too late
Even for thy consoling to revive.

IX.

She pass'd out of my youth at the still time
    O' the early light, when all was green and husht.
She pass'd, and pass'd away. Like broken rhyme
    Her sweet short life's few relics are. This crusht
And scatter'd rose, she dropp'd: that page, she
        turn'd,
    And finish'd not: this curl, her gift: this knot
    That flutter'd from her . . . Hard world, harm
        them not!
My right to keep them hath been sorely earn'd.

DROPPINGS.

I.

THE leaves that fall on the grassy wall,
  And the rain dropping out of the apple tree!
And is it only a passing dream?
For I know not why, but these things seem
  Just now worth more than the world to me.

II.

Fast the leaves fall on the grassy wall;
  Fast drops the rain from the apple tree;
And if I could feel what I feel now
But a moment longer, I think I should know
  More than ever was known, or known will be.

III.

Wherefore? Leaves fall all day on the wall,
  All day drops rain from the apple tree.
But never before did the leaves and the rain,
And they doubtless will never, never again,
  Seem about to impart such a secret to me.

IV.

Mere leaves that fall on yonder wall!
  Mere rain dropping down out of yonder tree!
What matter? If Nature has something to say,
Let her take her own time, let her choose her own
      way,
  So long as at last she will say it to me.

V.

Ah! but leaves will fall, as now, on the wall
　　And rain, as now, drop from out of the tree,
Many, many a day, while the chance, I know,
Is lost! I have miss'd what, a moment ago,
　　The leaves and the rain had confided to me.

———

ΓΝΩΘΙ ΣΕΑΤΤΟΝ.

WELL and good is this doctrine of " Know thyself,"
And let him obey it, that can, to the letter;
Self-ignorance being the veriest fetter
That ever kept fools in the stocks, no doubt.
But, while the Greek sages lie there on my shelf,
Why should I scruple to speak my mind out,
And assert that " Forget thyself " is a better?
Self-unconsciousness being, perchance,
The one thing free from self-ignorance.
Not by looking within, but by living without,
This centre of self, shall a man grow wise.
Let us, leaving ourselves, then, go boldly about,
And take part in the business of earth and skies:
For only by knowledge of that which is not
Thyself, shall thyself be learn'd, I wot.
Woe to the nation, and woe to the age, and woe, woe
　　to the man
That live not outside of themselves! To them dis-
　　solution is near.
Healthful and happy are they that, promoting the
　　infinite plan,
Are moved with the movement of things, and have joy
　　in the general cheer.

KNOWLEDGE AND WISDOM.

MEASURE thy knowledge by the weight of it,
  Which is a kind of sorrowfulness.   Men
  Dig deep, get gold, and judge its value then,
According as the heaviness be great of it.

But love thy wisdom for the lightness of it.
  Glad wisdom is not gotten, but is given:
  Not dug out of the earth, but dropp'd from
      Heaven:
Heavenly, not earthly, is the brightness of it.

————

SIDE BY SIDE.   .

I.

(FRIEND AND FRIEND.)

MAY we, then, never know each other?
  Who love each other more, I dare
Affirm for both, than brother brother,
  Ay! more, my friend, than they that are
      The children of one mother.

A look—and lo, our natures meet!
  A word—our minds make one reply!
A touch—our hearts have but one beat!
  And, if we walk together—why
      The same thought guides our feet

The self-same course!   The flower that blows
　A scent unguess'd in hedgerow green,
Slim spiders, where the water throws,
　The starry-weeded stones between,
　　Strange light that flits and flows,

Were charged by some sweet spirit, sure,
　(Love's minister, and ours!) to strike
Our sense with one same joy, allure
　Our hearts, and bless us both alike
　　With memories that endure.

True friend!   I know you : and I know
　You know me too.   And this is well.
Yet something seems to lie below
　All knowledge, which is hard to tell.
　　The world, where hands let go,

Slips in between.   The warmth yet stays
　Where, twelve safe hours ago, no more
Your soul touch'd mine.   But days and days
　Make callous what one day leaves sore,
　　Ichoring the wound they graze.

Not ours the change, if change must fall,
　Nor yours the fault, nor mine, my friend!
Life's love will last : but not love's small
　Sweet hourly lives.   That these should end
　　It grieves me.   That is all.

This is time's curse.   Since life began
　It hath been losing love too fast.

And I would keep, while yet I can,
　Man's faith in love, lest at the last
　　I lose love's faith in man.

But something sighs, "Be satisfied.
　Ye know no more than ye can know."
And walking, talking, side by side,
　It sometimes seems to me as though
　　Love did to love provide

(How shall I say?) a man, in fine,
　A ghostly Third,—who is, indeed,
Not you nor I, though yours and mine;
　The creature of our mutual need,
　　The friend for whom we pine.

You call him Me: I call him You:
　Who is not either you nor I:
This phantom friend, whom we pursue,
　Released by Love's fine alchemy,
　　Mere product of us two!

The man that each in each hath sought,
　And each within himself hath found:
The being of our separate thought,
　To each by his own nature bound,
　　From his own nature wrought.

Heed well our friend, while yet we may!
　There are so many winds about,
And any wind may blow away
　Love's airy child.　O never doubt
　　He is the common prey

Of every chance, while love remains:
  And every chance, which he survives
Is something added to love's gains.
  Comfort our friend whilst yet he lives!
    Dead, what shall pay our pains?

If cold should kill his heart at last,
  Regret will idly muse, and think
In at what window blew the blast?
  Or how we might have stopp'd that chink.
    What mends a moment past?

II.

(MAN AND WIFE.)

Nay, Sweet! no thought, not any thought,
  At least not any thought of you,
But what must thank dear love.   Nor aught
  Of love's mistrust between us two
Can ever creep.   Thank God, we keep
  Too close to let thin doubts slip through,

And leave a scar where they divide
  Hearts meant by Heaven to hold together.
So, soul by soul, as side by side,
  We sit.   Thought wanders hither, thither,
From star to star, yet not so far
  But what, at end of all its tether,

It feels the beating of your heart,
  To which mine bound it long ago.
Our love is perfect, every part.

Love's utmost reach'd at last, must so
Henceforth abide.   And, if I sigh'd
Just now, I scarcely wish to know

The reason why.   Who feels love's best,
  Must feel love's best can be no more.
We see the bound, no longer guess'd,
  But fix'd for ever.   Lo, the shore!
On either hand, 'twixt sea and land,
  How clear and fine does sight explore

That long-drawn self-determined line
  Of difference traced!   My Own, forgive
That, sitting thus, your hand in mine,
  Glad that dear God doth let us live
So close, my Own, so almost one,
  A thought that wrongs repose should strive

With pure content.   So much we are,
  Who are no more . . . . could I explain!
Ah, the calm sea-coast!   Think, how far
  Across the world came land and main,
Endeavouring each to find and reach
  The other,—well, and they attain

Here!   And just here, where they unite,
  The point of contact seems to be
The point of severance.   Left and right,
  Here lies the land and there the sea.
They meet from far: they touch: yet are
  Still one and one eternally,

With still that touch between—that touch
   That joins and yet divides—the shore.
Oh soul to soul, dear love, 'tis much!
   Love's utmost gain'd can give no more.
And yet . . . Well, no! 'tis better so.
   Earth still (be glad!) holds Heaven in store.

DIVIDED LIVES.

O LIVES beloved, wherein mine once did live,
   Thinking your thoughts, and walking in your ways,
   On your dear presence pasturing all my days,
In pleasantness, and peace ; whose moods did give
The measure to mine own ! how vainly strive
   Poor Fancy's fingers, numb'd by time, to raise
   This veil of woven years, that from my gaze
To hide what now you are doth still contrive !
Dear lives, I marvel if to you yet clings
   Of mine some colour; and my heart then feels
Much like the ghost of one who died too young
   To be remember'd well, that sometimes steals
A family of unsad friends among
   Sighing, and hears them talk of other things.

SACRIFICE.

UNTO my soul I said—"Make now complete
Thy sacrifice by silence.   Undeterr'd,
Strike down this beggar heart, that would be heard,
And stops men's pity in the public street;
A mendicant for miserable meat !
Nor pay thy vassal, Pain, with any word,
Lest so the deed thou docst should be slurr'd
By shameful recompense, and all unsweet.
Uncover not the faces of thy dead.
Slay thy condemnèd self, and hide the knife.
And even as death, compassionating life,
With gracious verdure doth the graves o'erspread,
So hide beneath a smiling face the whole
Of thine unutter'd misery, O my soul !"

DUTY.

How like a trumpet from the sentinel
Angel, that standeth in the morning star,
Empanoplied and plumed, as angels are
Whom God doth charge to watch that all be well,
Cometh to me thy call, O terrible,
That, girt, and crown'd, and sworded for Heaven's
    war,
Standest supreme above the confused jar
Of shock'd antagonisms, and the yell
Of trampled pain ! Thou of the solemn eyes,
Firm-fronted Duty, on whose high command
My heart waits awed, stretch forth thy harness'd
    hand,
And with a louder summons bid arise
My soul to battle. Hark, the muster-roll !
Thy name is call'd. Forth, thou poor conscript soul !

From "*FABLES IN SONG.*"

INTRODUCTORY.

I.

A LITTLE bird fares well in Spring.
   For all she wants she finds enough,
And every casual common thing
   She makes her own without rebuff.

II.

First, wool and hair from sheep and cow:
   Then twig and straw, to bind them fast,
From thicket and from thatch: and now
   A little nest is built at last.

III.

From out that little nest shall rise,
   When woods are warm, a living song,
A music mixt with light, that flies
   Thro' fluttering shade the leaves among.

IV.

Its home? straw, twig, and wool, and hair.
    Mere nothings, these, to house or herd.
Who made them something, made them fair,
    Making them all her own?   The bird.

V.

O little bird, take everything,
    And build thy nest without rebuff,
And, when thy nest is builded, sing!
    For who can praise thy song enough?

VI.

And some believe (believe they wrong?)
    If like the bird the bard could sing,
That, like the bird, fit home for Song
    The bard would find in everything.

VII.

By casual grace of common chance
    From house and herd, from thick and thatch,
Assign'd for Song's inheritance
    Had Song the gift that grace to catch.

VIII.

Such things I found, by passers-by
    As rubbish from the roadside thrust;
Which poets, seeking poesy,
    Disdain'd to rescue from the dust.

IX.

Yet here they are—not rubbish now
  I fain would hope.   Do critics stare,
Reserve applause, and rub the brow?
  O that a little bird I were!

————

THE THISTLE. Motto.

(A FLOWER'S BALLAD.)

IT was a thorn,
  And it stood forlorn
In the burning sunrise land:

A blighted thorn,
  And at eve and morn
Thus it sigh'd to the desert sand.

" Every flower,
  By its beauty's power,
With a crown of glory is crown'd.

No crown have I,
  For a crown I sigh,
For a crown that I have not found.

A crown! a crown!
  A crown of mine own,
To wind in a maiden's hair!"

Sad thorn, why grieve?
Thou a crown shalt weave,
But not for a maiden to wear.

That crown shall shine
When all crowns save thine,
With the glory they gave, are gone;

For, thorn, my thorn,
Thy crown shall be worn
By the King of Sorrows alone.

PRELUDE.

The green grass-blades aquiver
  With joy at the dawn of day
(For the most inquisitive ever
  Of the flowers of the field are they)
Lisp'd it low to their lazy
  Neighbours that flat on the ground,
Dandelion and daisy,
  Lay still in a slumber sound:
But soon, as a ripple of shadow
  Runs over the whisperous wheat,
The rumour ran over the meadow
  With its numberless fluttering feet:
It was told by the water-cresses
  To the brooklet that, in and out
Of his garrulous green recesses,
  For gossip was gadding about:
And the brooklet, full of the matter,
  Spread it abroad with pride;

But he stopp'd to gossip and chatter,
  And turn'd so often aside,
That his news got there before him
  Ere his journey down was done;
And young leaves in the vale laugh'd o'er him,
  "We know it! *The snow is gone!*"

The snow is gone! but ye only
Know how good doth that good news sound,
  Whose hearts, long buried and lonely,
Have been waiting, winter-bound,
  For the voice of the wakening angel
  To utter the welcome evangel,
"The snow is gone: re-arise,
  And blossom as heretofore,
Hopes, imaginings, memories,
  And joys of the days of yore!"

'Tis the white anemone, fashion'd so
Like to the stars of the winter snow,
First thinks, "If I come too soon, no doubt
  I shall seem but the snow that hath staid too
    long,
So 'tis I that will be Spring's unguess'd scout."
  And wide she wanders the woods among.
The borage, blue-eyed, with a thrill of pride,
(For warm is her welcome on every side)
From Elfland coming to claim her place,
  Garments gay of green velvet takes
Creased from the delicate travelling case
  A warm breeze breaks. The daisy awakes
And opens her wondering eyes, yet red

About the rims with a too long sleep;
Whilst, bold from his ambush, with helm on head
   And lance in rest, doth the bulrush leap.
Primrose and violet nestle themselves,
Under the trees, by tens and twelves.
But the venturous cowslips, one by one,
   Trembling, chilly, atiptoe stand
On little hillocks and knolls alone;
   Watchful pickets, that wave a hand
For signal sure that the snow is gone,
   Then around them call their comrades all
   In many a blithe and festal band;
Till the field is alive with grass and flowers,
   And wherever the flashing footsteps fall,
Of the fleet, ethereal April showers,
The untoucht earth laughs, overlaid
With multitudinous blossom and blade.

PART I.

'Twas long after the grass and the flowers, one
      day,
That there came straggling along the way
   A little traveller, somewhat late.
   Tired he was; and down he sat
In the ditch by the road, where he tried to nestle
   Out of the dust and the noontide heat.
Poor little vagabond wayside Thistle!
   In the ditch was his only safe retreat.
Flung out of the field as soon as found there,
   And banisht the garden, where should he stay?
Wherever he roam'd, still Fortune frown'd there,
   And, wherever he settled, spurn'd him away.

From place to place, had he wander'd long
 The weary high road, parcht with thirst.
Now here, in the ditch, for awhile among
 The brambles hidden, he crouch'd; and first
  Wistfully eyed, on the other side,
A fresh green meadow with flow'rets pied;
And then, with a pang, as he peep'd and pried,
 " Oh, to rest there!" he thought, and sigh'd.
 . " Oh, to rest there, it is all so fair!
Yonder wanders a brooklet, sure?
No! it is only the mill-sluice small.
But he looks like a brook, so bright and pure,
 And his banks are broider'd with violets all.
  Soft!—I have half a mind to try—
Could one slip in yonder quietly,
Where the rippled damp of the deep grass spares
 Cool rest to each roving butterfly,
How pleasant 'twould be! There is nobody by,
 And perhaps there is nobody owns or cares
To look after yon meadow. It seems so still,
Silent, and safe—shall I venture?—I will!
 From the ditch it is but a step or two.
And, maybe, the owner is dead, and the heirs
 Away in the town, and will never know."

PART II.

Then the little Thistle atiptoe stood,
 All in a tremble, sharp yet shy.
The vagabond's conscience was not good.
 He had been so often a trespasser sly,
He had been so often caught by the law,
 He had been so often beaten before;
He was still so small: if a spade he saw,
 He mutter'd a *Paternoster* o'er,

And cower'd. So, cautiously thrusting out
Here a timorous leaf, there a tiny sprout,
And then dropping a seed, and so waiting anon
For a chance lift got from the wind—still on,
With a hope that the sun and the breeze might
  please
To be helpful and kind—by degrees he frees
And feels his way with a fluttering heart.
 In the ditch there were heaps of stones to pass.
They scratch'd him, and tore him, and made him
  smart,
 And ruin'd his leaves. But those leaves, alas,
Already so tatter'd and shatter'd were,
 That to keep them longer was worth no care;
And at last he was safe in the meadow; and there
 "Ah, ha!" sigh'd the Thistle; "so far, so
  well!
If I can but stay where I am, I shall fare
 Blithe as the bee in the blossom's bell.
O blest abode! To have done with the road,
And got rid of the ditch! Ah, who can tell
 The rapture of rest to the wanderer's breast?"
 Down out of heaven a dewdrop fell
On the head of the Thistle: and he fell asleep
In the lap of the twilight soft and deep.

PART III.

At sunrise he woke: and he still was there,
 In the bright grass, breathing the balmy air.
He stretch'd his limbs, and he shook off the dust,
 And he wash'd himself in the morning dew;
And, opening his pedlar's pack, out-thrust
 A spruce little pair of leaflets new;
And made for himself a fine white ruff,

About his neck to wear;
And pruned and polish'd his prickles tough;
  And put on a holiday air.
And " If only nobody finds me out! "
  He laugh'd, as he loll'd among
The grass, delighted, and look'd about,
  And humm'd a homely song,
  In his wanderings heard elsewhere—

> " *A crown! a crown!*
> *A crown of mine own,*
> *To wind in a maiden's hair!* "

But . . . a sweep of the scythe, and a stamp of the
    foot,
  And " Vile weed! is there no getting rid of thee
    ever? "
And what little was spared by the scythe, the boot,
  With its hobnails, hasten'd to crush and shiver.

PART IV.

'Twas the Farmer, who just then happen'd to pass.
He had gone to the field to cut some grass
For his beast that morn; and no sooner saw
  The trespasser there *in flagrante delicto*,
Than, scythe in hand, he enforced the law
  On the luckless offender, *vi et ictu*.

All mangled and bruised, the poor little Thistle
  With his desperate roots to the soil clung fast.
The Farmer away, with a careless whistle,
  Homeward over the meadow pass'd.

The Thistle breathed freer, and shook his gasht head.
   "All's well, if it be no worse!" he said.
"My crown is gone, but 'twill grow again.
   There is many another (*I feel it*) in me.
And one must not make too much of the pain.
   Only, you good saints, let me not be
Forced, for my sins, to return to the road!"
Then his roots he burrow'd more deep and broad.

But every day 'twas the self-same thing!
   Tho' he made himself little, and hid his head,
Trying, with all his might, to cling
   Close to the soil, and appear to be dead.
For his spacious leaves, that were carved and curl'd.
   For Corinthian columns in temples fair,
He could not check them when these unfurl'd
   Their flourishing architecture there,
And, all about him their beauty spreading,
   Layer upon layer uprose from below;
And the hardy young head, in despite of beheading,
   Sprang up again—for the scythe to mow!
Round and about him, each blossom was blowing.
No chance of blowing had *he* found ever:
Who no sooner was seen than the sharp steel
      mowing,
Or the harsh foot crushing him, stopp'd the
      endeavour.
And, "Oh, blessèd," he sigh'd, "is the blossom
      that blows!
   Colours I know of, no eyes yet see.
But I dare not show them; and nobody knows,
   Nobody guesses, what's hidden in me!
   In all the world but one creature, alas,
For love's sake seeks me; and *he* is an ass."

PART V.

So went the Spring: and so came and went
  The Summer.   The aftermath was mown.
In bristly patches, no longer blent
  With the glow of the blossoms that there had
    blown,
The lean gaunt herbage scantly grew,
  And the beast of the field had the residue
    The primrose was gone, and the violet,
And under the desolate woods, the white
  Anemone's constellations, set,
  Had left the earth dark as a starless night,
    But, outliving his betters one by one,
In the flowerless field, with no thought of flight,
  The brave little Thistle remain'd—alone!
    And, since skies were cold, and suns were dim,
No one noticed, and no one praised,
  But also no one *maltreated*, him.
And the pensive beasts of the field, that grazed
  The twice-cropt grass, where their wandering
    whim
    Led them, lazy, from spot to spot,
Shunn'd the Thistle and harm'd him not.

PART VI.

Then the Thistle, at last, could enlarge his store
Of the few joys fate had vouchsafed him sparely.
  Baffled a hundred times, and more,
  Bruised, and torn, and surviving barely,
Still he *survived:* and for him, him only,
  Green leaves gladden'd the leafless cold

Where, Summer's orphan, he linger'd lonely
   Over her grave in the frozen mould.
For, as days, long dead, by a bard born after
   Are invoked, and revive in a form more fair,
All the bliss that was beauty, the life that was
      laughter,
   Ere the frolic fields were bereft and bare,
The lone Thistle renew'd and transform'd to his
      own;
   As flower by flower—from the fervid rose,
Whose beauty so well to herself is known,
   That she blushes proud of the truth she knows,
To the violet, Modesty's vanquisht child,
   Hiding her head in the sylvan places
Where her wandering wooer, the March gust wild,
   Hath left her faint from his harsh embraces,
     All of them—all, in a dream divine
To the Thistle their else-lost secrets told
     Of blushes that burn, and of brows that shine,
      With passion of purple and glory of gold.
So all flowers of the field were alive in one:
     And the glow of his sheen, and the gloss of his
      down,
Were as jewels dead queens have confided alone
To the craftsman who fashions them all to a crown.

For each hope in the heart of the poor plant hidden,
   Each vision of bliss and of beauty, nurst
With a passion, by Prejudice check'd and chidden,
   For a life by the fiat of Fortune curst,
Rushing forthwith into rich reality,
   Fill'd the cup of a quenchless thirst
Till it flow'd with exuberant prodigality,
   And his long-pent life into blossom burst.

A single blossom: but statelier far,
And fairer, than many a million are.
A splendid disc, full and flashing with wonder!
    As the sea-rose swims on the water, so
That effulgent star on the bleak earth under
    Lay spread out in a luminous glow.
And " At last I can blossom! blossom! blossom!"
    The Thistle laugh'd, greeting the earth and
        heaven,
And he blossom'd his whole heart out of his bosom,
    And all was forgotten, save all that was given.

———

POSSESSION.

A POET loved a Star,
    And to it whisper'd nightly,
" Being so fair, why art thou, love, so far?
Or why so coldly shine, who shinest so brightly?
    O Beauty, woo'd and unpossest,
    O might I to this beating breast
    But clasp thee once, and then die, blest!"

That Star her Poet's love,
    So wildly warm, made human,
And, leaving for his sake her heaven above,
His Star stoop'd earthward, and became a woman.
    " Thou who hast woo'd and hast possest,
    My lover, answer, which was best,
    The Star's beam, or the Woman's breast?"

" I miss from heaven," the man replied,
  " A light that drew my spirit to it."
And to the man the woman sigh'd,
  " I miss from earth a poet."

———

PREMATURITY.

I.

IF aught in Nature be unnatural,
  It is the slaying by a spring-tide frost
Of Spring's own children: cheated blossoms all,
Betray'd i' the birth, and born for burial
  Of budding promise, scarce beloved ere lost!
Once, in the silence of a clear Spring night,
This still, cold-footed Frost, with footstep light
  Slid thro' the tepid season like a ghost
      Wrapt in thin white.
Flitting, he smote the first-born of the year,
And, ere the break of day, their pretty buds were
  sere.

II.

  But the blossoms that perish'd
    Were those alone
  Which, in haste to be cherish'd
    With loosen'd zone
Had too soon to the sun all their beauty shown.
    Lightly-vested,
    Amorous-breasted,

Blossom of almond, blossom of peach:
Impatient children, with hearts unsteady,
So young and yet more precocious each
Than the leaves of the Summer, and blushing
already!

III.

These perish'd, because too soon they lived;
But the oak-flower, prudent and proud, survived.
"If the sun would win me," she thought, "he
must
Wait for me, wooing me warmly the while;
For a flower's a fool, if a flower would trust
Her whole sweet being to one first smile."

THE FAR AND THE NEAR.

(TO E. L.)

FAIR soul, that o'er mine own dost shine
So fair, so far above,
Dear heart, that hast so close to mine
The home of thy true love:

Be thine these songs of Far and Near!
Two worlds their sources are:
Each makes the other doubly dear,
The near one and the far.

THE BLUE MOUNTAINS; OR, THE FAR.

PART I.

I.

When little kings, whose race was run
    A little while ago,
Had little thrones to sit upon,
    And little else to do,
Within a little town, remote
    From Europe's larger scenes,
There dwelt a man of little note,
    Who lived on little means.

II.

A man, he was, of humble birth and mind,
    His life was lowly, small was his estate.
Yet was there ever a human life confined
    In bounds so narrow by ungenerous fate,
But it had in it something far and strange?
    This man, from youth to age, had lived and grown
In a great longing for a far blue range
    Of hills that hover'd o'er his native town.
Ne'er had his footsteps climb'd those mountains blue,
    But half his life, and all his thoughts, dwelt there.
He was a man beyond himself.   They drew
    His being out of him, and made it fair.
For wheresoe'er his gaze around him roved,
    There were those beautiful blue hills.   And he,
Who lived, not in himself, but them, so loved
    And so revered them, that they ceased to be
To him mere hills, mere human feet may wend.
    Their azure summits, to his longing view,
Were features of a dear, though distant friend,
    In kingly coronal and mantle blue.

III.

And " Oh," he mused, "full sure am I
Those mountains feel, in silent joy,
The love my gaze doth give them.   They
Seek it, indeed, with signs all day ;
Down drawing o'er their shoulders fair,
This way and that, soft veils of air,
And colours, never twice the same,
Woven of wind, and dew, and flame,
And strange cloud-shadows, and slant showers.

" That is their speech.   'Tis unlike ours,
Easy to learn, tho', if one tries ;
One only has to use his eyes.
The colours are the vowels.   These
Are liquid links whose mobile ease
Such fluent combination grants
To those substantial consonants,
Precipitous crags, and sudden peaks.
The accents are the lightning-streaks
And thunder-claps, that render, each,
Such emphasis to mountain speech.
Next follow fog and mist, which are
Verbs we may call irregular ;
Perplexing when at first you view them,
But persevere, and you'll get thro' them.
Then comes the rain, which just supplies
The necessary quantities
Of notes of admiration.   Far
Too many, folks may think they are.
But if such folks could understand
The mountains, there on every hand
They'd find about them more, far more,
Than notes of admiration, score

On score, suffice for. Think, what lands
And peoples every peak commands !
Then find the statesman that knows how
To govern one land. As for two,
That task's beyond the best, we feel.
Now, had we, like the hills, to deal
With winds, and storms, and clouds, and snows,
Nor lose our dignified repose,
Who'd wonder why the hills abound
In thoughts so serious, so profound,
About what men, when met together,
Talk, without thinking, of—the weather ?
But still to talk it is men's wont,
Both when they think and when they don't.
Ah, good old hills! If majesty
Should, some day hence, be forced to fly
From all her other thrones on earth,
'Tis there, with you, who gave her birth,
That she her latest home would find,
Above, but still *among*, mankind ! "

PART II.

I.

Thus ever the fancies of the man
(Like their own restless rills)
Upon the mighty mountains ran,
Refresht by far-off hills.
Not one of his neighbours, he could swear,
Half so well as those mountains, knew him,
Who wrapp'd his soul in their robe of blue.
And, if that were fancy, *this* was true :

That, whether or not, those mountains fair
For the good of this man had a thought or care,
Much good they had contrived to do him
By simply being there.

II.

His only wish was to tell them of it,
And requite them for it.   But not, as now,
When to every peak, with the snow above it,
And the azure of heaven above the snow,
It was only his wishes that found their way;
But among the hills, *himself*, some day
Before he died, if that might be,
When the hills could hear what he had to say,
And how much to say to the hills had he !

III.

Oh, heavenly power of human wishes
For as wings to birds, and as fins to fishes,
Are a man's desires to the soul of a man.
'Tis by these, and by these alone, it can
Wander at will thro' its native sphere
Where the beauty that's far is the bliss that is near.
Fate favour'd the wishes of this poor man.
For the wave of the ebbing century ran
In a sudden surge of storm at last
Over the little spot of earth,
Where, else, unnoticed he might have past
To his obscure death from his obscure birth.
And thus he, whose life had lain out of sight,
A social nothing, the strain and swell
Of the time's strong trouble swept into light,

And suddenly made perceptible.
Then, as soon as noticed by those in power,
The man was honour'd (O happy hour!)
By the sight of his name in a Royal Decree;
Which inform'd the world that he (poor *he*!
Who could have fancied so strange a thing?)
Had really and truly lived to be
A cause of alarm to his lord the King.
For it banish'd him to a place, he knew
Must be in the midst of those mountains blue.
And thus his wishes, at last, came true.

PART III.

I.

Glad was our friend, when himself he found,
In travelling trim, to the mountains bound!
The way was long, and the road was steep,
And, before he had got to his journey's end,
The night was dark, and the hills asleep.
"Aha!" thought he, "will they know their friend,
Who is here at last? Too late to-night
To see them, of course! They are sleeping now.
But to-morrow, to-morrow at earliest light,
I shall arise ere the red cock crow,
And visit mine old friends, every one."

II.

So, at dawn, he arose with the rising sun,
And forth, as blithe as a bird, went he.
At first he was puzzled and pain'd, to find
All round him a field which appear'd to be

719

Just like the fields he had left behind:
A little meadow of grass, hemm'd round
With many a little hillock and mound,
Which hinder'd his sight from ranging far.
"But soon are these small hills climbed," he thought,
" And behind them, doubtless, the blue ones are,
Where, sportively hiding, they wish to be caught."

III.

Then he mounted the hillocks that rose close by,
And thence, indeed, he beheld once more
The old blue hills.   But they were not nigh;
They were far, far, far away, as before.

IV.

"Strange!" he mused, "yet I travell'd all day,
Ay, and more than the half o' the night, too, post!
And all my life I have heard folks say
That the blue hills are but a day, at most,
From my native town.   Did they err, I wonder?"
Then he askéd of a traveller passing by,
" Pray, sir, what is that country yonder?
There, where the hills are so blue and high."
And, when the traveller had told him the name
Of the place where the blue hills now were seen,
Alas, poor man! 'twas the very same
Where, till then, he had all his life long been :
The country about his native town—
His birthplace—whence he had just been banish'd.
The blue hills *there* he had never known,
And the blue hills *here*, which he loved, had
    vanish'd.

PART IV.

I.

" And have I been living, then, all this while
In a blue land—really and truly blue ? "
The exile sigh'd with a sorrowful smile,
" And never dream'd of it !   Can it be true?
Never dream'd of it !   All seem'd grey,
Or dusty white, with a patch or two
Of lean green grass, or raw red clay,
To enliven the rest.   But blue ? . . . blue ? . . .
 blue ? " . . .

II.

The man fell into a reverie.
O'er his cerulean home a brood
Of ethereal clouds were floating free.
And they sign'd to him, and he understood.

III.

" As the waves that are clad in the azure of ocean,
 So clad in the azure of heaven are we.
As thou movest, we move, with an unseen motion;
 And, where thou followest, there we flee.
For the children of Never and Ever we are,
And our home is Beyond, and our name is Afar.

" Never to us shall thy steps attain,
 Nor ever to thee may we draw nearer.
But, if fair in thy vision our forms remain,
 Still love us, the farther we are, the dearer,
And be thou ours, as thine we are,
For what were the near, were it not for the far ?

"Look above, and below—to the heaven, the plain!
　　The low and the level, they disappear.
The aloof and the lofty alone remain.
　　And, for ever present tho' never near,
Whilst ours are the summit, the sky, and the star
Still thine is the beauty of all that we are."

IV.

All this, in his much-loved mountain-tongue,
The man's heart, hearing it, understood.
And he thought of the old old days, so young!
But he spake not : only, let fall a flood
Of passionate notes of admiration,
Over his wan cheek silently sweeping.
As when, in their sorrow and desolation,
At the death of the summer, the hills are weeping.

V.

Then the folk about him, who knew not aught
Of that mountain language, shook the head.
"How he taketh his sentence to heart!" each
　　thought.
And "Courage! the time must mend," they said.

A WHEAT-STALK; OR, THE NEAR.

I.

THE cattle tinkle down the lanes,
　　And there the bramble-roses blow.
From rocky haunts to reach the plains
　　The rills, with shaken timbrel, go,

Gay dancers light!
The hills are bright
With gleaming peaks of golden snow.

By fragrant gales in frolic play
  The floating corn's green waves are fann'd,
And all above, broad summer day!
  And all below, bright summer land!
      And, born of each,
      Far out of reach,
Those shining alpine spectres stand.

II.

A world of beauty, grandeur, grace,
  Abundance, fill'd with force divine,
No sooner doth mine eye embrace
  Than my soul hath made it mine.
      How deep, O soul,
        Thy depth must be,
      To hold the whole
        Of a world in thee!

III.

But O eye, and O soul, is your thirst yet sated?
  Or what more do ye claim for your own?
Must this world, at the best, be so lightly rated,
  For the sake of a better, unknown?

Ah, farther away than the farthest hill-top
  Do I *feel* mine own boundless emotion!
And my heart, tho' o'erbrimm'd it may be by a
      drop,
  Is contented not with an ocean.

IV.

On the blossomy lattice ledge,
   Whence, far off, I descry
The long land's light blue edge,
   With, beyond it, but the sky,
From a glass half fill'd with water
   Leans an ear of wheat—a prize
Erewhile my little daughter
   Brought home with brighten'd eyes.
To her things near and known,
   Seem strange and far away,
The hamlet next our own
   As distant as Cathay!
Nor needs she earth should be
   So wondrous wide and far,
Such worlds at hand hath she,
   And every world a star!

V.

Why, dreaming ever, clings my gaze so fast
   To this small wheat-stem?   Whence its power
     to draw
My refluent thoughts from yonder distance vast,
   And hang them on a homely wheaten straw?

It is that, small and homely though it be,
   This ear of wheat so homely and so small,
Because it is so near, so near to me,
   Hath size enough and power to cover all.
It leans along full twenty leagues of land,
   And hides them with a straw.   The purple hills
Peer through its hoary panicle.   The grand
   Horizon's azure orb one wheat-stem fills.

Kindly perspective! Little things close by
  Exceed great things remote: for Nature's art
Brings vision to a centre in the eye,
  Affection to a centre in the heart.
And, were it not so, light and love would be
  Lost wanderers; and the universal frame
A heap of fragments; and the force to see,
  The force to feel, mere force without an aim.

VI.

O near ones, dear ones! you, in whose right hands
  Our own rests calm; whose faithful hearts all day
Wide open wait till back from distant lands
  Thought, the tired traveller, wends his homeward
    way!
Helpmates and hearthmates, gladdeners of gone
    years,
  Tender companions of our serious days,
Who colour with your kisses, smiles, and tears
  Life's warm web woven over wonted ways,

Young children, and old neighbours, and old friends,
  Old servants—you, whose smiling circle small
Grows slowly smaller till at last it ends
  Where in one grave is room enough for all,
O shut the world out from the heart you cheer!
  Tho' small the circle of your smiles may be,
The world is distant, and your smiles are near.
  This makes you more than all the world to me.

———

LOST TREASURES.

PART I.

IT was the splendid winter-tide,
And all the land was thrilling white,
In a solemn and songless sunshine wide,
Whose gorgeous uncongenial light
Harden'd whatever it glorified.
And while that glory was streaming amber
Into a childhood-haunted chamber,
A child, at play by the lattice-sill,
Where daily the redbreasts begging came,
Noticed a glittering icicle
That flash'd in the sun like a frozen flame.
So, plucking it off, he seized and put it
Into a box of gilded paper.
There, to be treasured for ever, shut it,
Danced about it with shout and caper,
And then, as a child will do, forgot it.
For suddenly under the lattice roll'd
A music of cymbal and trumpet blent.
And, oh merry and brave it was to behold
The soldiers below, who in scarlet and gold
Marching blithe to the music went.
And after the soldiers, cleaving the cold
Slantwise, shot like a falling arrow,
And perch'd on the sill of the lattice, a bold,
Bright-eyed, sharp-beak'd, hungry sparrow;
Claiming, with saucy, sidelong head,
His accustom'd alms of a crumb of bread,
Tho' to get what he ask'd he would not stop,
But off, with a pert, impatient hop,
Went twittering over the roof instead.

Next follow'd far more than a man can mention
Of indoor claims on a child's attention.
And at last 'twas a whip to whip the top,
And "Oh, where is Grandfather? 'tis he must
　　find one!"
Then away in a hurry the small feet trot,
Yet pause: for that icicle, first forgot,
And then remember'd all in a minute,
It were surely a pity to leave behind one.　.
So the treasure-box, with the treasure in it,
Their tiny treasurer carries away.
But ah, what sorrowful change is this
In the box where safely the bright gem lay
Erewhile, a secretly-beaming bliss
To beautify many a winter's day?
For, drop by drop, is the drench'd box dripping,
And the gilded paper is all undone,
And, away in a shower of warm tears slipping,
The deceitful treasure is well-nigh gone.
So, weeping too, with the woeful story
(In a passion of grief unreconciled
For the lost delight of a vanisht glory)
To the old man hastens the troubled child.

PART II.

Lone by the old hearth was the old man sitting.
He, too, a treasure-box had on his knee;
And slowly, slowly, like sad snow-flakes flitting
Down from the weak boughs of a wither'd tree,
Fell from his tremulous fingers, wet with tears,
Into the embers of the old hearth's fire,
Wan leaves of paper yellow'd by long years:
Letters, that once were treasures.

The Grandsire
Welcomed the infant with a kind, faint smile.
The burning letters, black and wrinkled, rose
Along the gusty flue; and there awhile
(Like one who, doubtful of the way he goes,
Lingers and hesitates) along the dark
They hover'd and delay'd their ghostly flight,
Thin sable veils wherein a restless spark
Yet trembled!—and then pass'd from human sight.
How oft had human eyes in days of yore
Above them beam'd, and with what tender light!
Wherefore, O wherefore, had those eyes no more
Upon them gazed for many a heedless year?
Was not the record which those eyes had read
With such bright rapture in each blissful tear
Still writ in the same letters, which still said
The self-same words?   Ah! why not now, as then,
With the same power to brighten those changed
    eyes?
Why should such looks such letters meet again
As strangers? each to each a sad surprise!
" How pale," the eyes unto the letters said,
" And wan, and weak, and yellow are ye grown!"
And to the eyes the letters, " Why so red
About the rims, and wrinkled?   Eyes unknown,
Nor ever seen before, to us ye seem,
Save for a something in the depths of you
Familiar to us, like a life-like dream
So well remember'd it almost seems true!"

The grandchild weeps upon the grandsire's knee,
And babbles of his treasure fled away.
The old man listens to him patiently,
And tells the child, as tho' great news were there,

Old tales which well the child already knows,
And smoothes his tumbled curls, and comforts him.
The winter day is darkening to its close,
On the old hearth the dying fire grows dim.

PART III.

The child upon the old man's breast was sleeping,
The old man stiller than the sleeping child!
Then slowly, softly, near and nearer creeping
From book-shelves dark, and dusty papers piled,
Old thoughts, old memories of the days of old,
Which lurk'd about that old room everywhere,
Hidden in many a curtain's quiet fold,
Panel, or picture-frame, or carven chair,
All silent, in the silence, one by one,
Came from between the long-unlookt-at leaves
Of old books; rose up from the old hearth-stone;
Descended from the old roof's oaken eaves;
Laid spectral hand in hand by twos and threes,
And then by tens and twenties; circled dim
Around the old man, on whose tranquil knees
Still slept the infant; and, saluting him,
The eldest whisper'd, "Dost thou know us not?
Many are we who come to take farewell.
For all departs at last. Ay, even the thought
Of what hath been. Sunbeam and icicle,
Childhood and age! The joys of childhood perish
Before the heats of manhood; manhood's heats
Before the chills of age. Whate'er ye cherish,
As whatsoe'er ye suffer, fades and fleets.
What goes not with the heat, goes with the cold.
For all that comes, goes also. What ye call
Life, is no more than dyings manifold.
All changes, all departs, all ends. All, all!"

ONLY A SHAVING.

I.

A CHILD, as from school he was bounding by,
Near the wall of a carpenter's workshop found
A lustrous shaving that lured his eye;
And this treasure he timidly pick'd from the ground.
The thing was tender, transparent, light,
Silk-soft, odorous, vein'd so fine
With rosy waves in the richest white,
Rare damask of dainty design!

II.

With awe he touch'd it, and turned it o'er.
He had never seen such a wonder before.
And, gay as a ringlet of golden hair,
It had floated and fallen down at his feet;
Where, fluttering faint in each breath of bright air,
It lay bathed by the sunshine sweet.

III.

The boy was a widow's sireless son.
A poor dame, pious and frugal, she.
Brothers and sisters he had none,
Playmates and playthings few: and he
Was gentle, and dreamy, and pure, as one
To whom most pleasures privations be
Ere childhood's playing is done.

IV.

He would like to have taken his treasure away.
" But what," he thought, " would my mother say?"

As he wistfully eyed the window'd wall
Whence down from the casement of some ground
    floor
He thought he had seen the fair thing fall.
Then he knock'd at the half-shut door.

v.

Near it the sturdy head workman stood.
He was busily planing a plank of wood.
His arms were up to the elbows bare,
Brawny and brown as the branch of an oak,
And heavy with muscle and dusky with hair.
Down over his forehead and face in a soak,
(For the heat of his labour had left them wet)
Fell mane-like, matted, and black as jet,
A huge unkempt and cumbrous coil
Of stubborn curls; that to forehead and face,
Gave a savage look as he stoop'd at his toil,
With many a sullen and sooty trace
Of the glue-pot's grease and the workshop's soil.
His shirt—last Sunday, though coarse, as clean
As the parson's own,—this Friday noon
Had the hue of the shift of that famous queen
Who took Granada, but not so soon
As her oath was taken.   This man had seen
The gentle child at the door, and thought
"'Tis the child of a customer come with a message.
"Pray, what has my little master brought?
Or what may he want?" With no cheerful presage
At the sight of his grim-faced questioner,
A few faint words the poor child stammers,
Words unheard 'mid the noisy stir
Of the hissing saws and the beating hammers.

When, abasht and blushing, he stands deterr'd
With a fluttering heart like a frighten'd bird;
As he holds the shaving out in his hand,
Timidly gazing at that strange prize.

VI.

The workman was puzzled to understand
This gracious vision.   He rubbed his eyes.
Is it vainly such visions come and go
In flashes across life's labouring way?
We uplift the forehead and fain would know
What to think of them.   Whence come they?
For they burst upon us and brighten the air
For a moment round us, and melt away,
Lost as we longingly look at them.

VII.

"Hi!
Silence, all of you hands down there!"
And you might have heard the hum of a fly
In the hush of the suddenly silenced place.
"What is it, my child?"   With a glowing face—
"Sir," said the child, "I was passing by,
And I saw it fall, as I pass'd below,
From the window, I think.   So, as it fell near,
I have pick'd it up, and I bring it you now."
"Bring what?"   "This beautiful ringlet here.
Have you not miss'd it?   It must, I know,
Have been hard to make.   I have taken care.
The wind was blowing it round the wall,
And I never saw anything half so fair.
But it is not broken, I think, at all."

VIII.

A 'prentice brat, whose cheek was puft
With a burst of laughter ready to split,
Turn'd pale, by a single glance rebuft
Of that workman's eye, which had noticed it.
And the man there, shaggy and black as a bear,
Nor any the sweeter for sweat and glue,
Laid a horny hand on the child's bright hair,
With a gentle womanly gesture drew
The child up softly on to his knees,
And gazed in its eyes till his own eyes grew
Humid and red at the iims by degrees.

IX.

"What is thine age, fair child?" he said.
"Five, next June."   "And it pleases thee,
This . . . ringlet-thing?"   The small bright head
Nodded.   He put the child from his knee,
Swept from the bench a whole curly clan
Of such shavings, and, "Hold up thy pinafore.
There, they are thine.   Run away, little man!"
"Mine?"   "All thine."   Then he open'd the door,
Stoop'd, and . . . was it a sigh or a prayer
That, as into the sunshine the sweet child ran,
Away with it pass'd in its golden hair?

X.

Anon, when the hubbub again began
Of hammer and saw in the workshop there,
This workman paused from his work; and stood
Looking awhile (as though vexed by the view)
At the shape which his work had bequeathed to the
    wood.

XI.

Then he turn'd him about, and abruptly drew
His pipe from his pocket, and stuff'd it, and lit,
And sat down on the bench by the open door,
And smoked, and smoked.   And in circles blue
As the faint smoke wander'd the warm air o'er,
Still he sat dreamily watching it
Rise like a ghost from the grimy clay,
And hover, and linger, and fade away.

XII.

I know not what were his thoughts.   But I know
There be shavings that down from a man's work fall,
Which the man himself, as they drop below,
Haply accounts of no worth at all ;
And I know there be children that prize them more
Than the man's true work, be its worth what it may,
And I think that (albeit 'twas not half o'er)
This workman turn'd from his work that day,
Having, just then, nor wish nor will
To go on planing a coffin still.

———

QUESTIONABLE CONSOLATION.

I.

A BUTTERFLY (and had the wretch been born
With all the beauties that, at best, adorn
   A butterfly's complete perfection, still
He but a butterfly had been, at best)

Came into life a cripple; dispossest
　Of half his natural features; born i' the chill,
Blemisht, and misbegotten; an abortion
Doom'd from the birth to suffering and distortion.

II.

One wing unfinisht, and misshapen one:
Six legs he had, but of his six legs none
　That served the purpose for which legs are made:
The piteous pivot of his own distress,
Aye with self-torturing unsteadiness
　About himself he turn'd; and found no aid
In aught that life vouchsafed him, leg or wing
To life's attainment of one wisht-for thing.

III.

He saw the others hovering in the sun;
He saw them seek each other; saw them shun
　Each other, by each other to be sought;
He saw them (each, itself, a second flower)
On flowers, entranced by the transcendent power
　Of their own happiness; he saw them, fraught
With frolic rapture, fearless wantons all!
And saw himself, unable even to crawl.

IV.

" And I," he thought, " I too, was meant to be
A wingèd joy, a wandering ecstasy!
　Ah, must I envy, for his happier lot,
The wingless worm that hath, complete, whate'er
As worm he wants; who wants no more, to fare
　Thro' life content; by life defrauded not
Of what mere life makes capable of joy
Even in a worm? still happier far than I!

V.

"I, to whom life refuses all things! all
Life's joy in earth, air, water! Still too tall
  The tiniest stem that bears the lowliest flower
For me to climb! too rough air's lightest sigh
For me to ride! the nearest dewdrop, dry
  Ere I can reach it! All, beyond my power!
All, save to disappear—go down—go by—
Sink out of life, not having lived—and die!"

VI.

The dying sun the insect's dying moan
O'erheard, and answer'd from his falling throne,
  "Mourn not! I, even I, the sun, go down,
Sink, and drop into darkness. Look at me!"
—He sinks. In pompous purple pillows he,
  His kingly forehead, girt with golden crown,
And, slowly, with delight his gaze grows dim,
Seeing earth's sadness for the loss of him.

VII.

Delicious homage of a dear dismay
Paid to the happy, when they pass away,
  By grief not theirs! Beneath him, prostrate, lies
A world that worships him; and everywhere
Therein he finds some record rich and fair
  Of his own power. He sinks: and wistful eyes
His pathway follow to its glorious bourn.
He sinks: and longing voices sigh "Return!"

VIII.

He passes: but he hath not pass'd in vain.
He passes, proving by life's loss its gain,
　　And bearing with him what he leaves behind.
He goes: rejoicing, "All that I have given
Memory makes mine again, and makes it even
　　Mine more completely than before.　I shined
Rising and setting.　All my light was shown,
And all my force was felt."　Thus suns go down.

IX.

The boastful orb's last glories, lingering,
That cripple smote.　"Go, glories! tell your king,"
　　Smiling, he said, "go, him that sent you tell,
Not all so wretched as I deem'd was I.
Since I have seen how suns go down, thereby
　　School'd have I been to know, and value well,
What they, the happy,—they that have it not,—
Would fain filch even from a wretch's lot,

X.

The grandeur of its utter desolation."
All glowing with rebuke and shamed vexation
　　The braggart sun's resentful blushes burst.
As o'er the deep, whose surface, and no more,
His glory gilt, he, slowly sinking, bore
　　This knowledge gain'd: that Misery at her worst
Hath one poor grace of tragic interest
Proud Pleasure vainly envies at his best.

From "*GLENAVERIL.*"

PART I., CANTO II.

I.

O youth, O childhood, fugitive angels you,
    That once, gone back to Heaven, return no more !
In vain our hearts invoke you to renew
    The joys that followed you ; in vain implore,
The bounty of a single drop of dew.
    That perisht with you from our paths before
We knew you gone.   The only dew that wets
Those pathways now falls there from vain regrets.

II.

Regrets that while you lingered here below,
    We knew not that ye would so soon depart,
Regrets that you are gone ; regrets to know
    That you will come no more ; regrets that start
To life at every backward glance we throw,
    Regrets that cling to the discouraged heart
When all the joys that smile on later years
Lost youth's *memento mori*, fills with tears.

III.

Oh, Heaven! to have been young, and all youth was,
    All we have felt and cannot feel again,
Still to remember and to find, alas,
    That the remembrance of lost joy is pain!
'Tis ever drinking from an empty glass.
    Better the full glass broken, than the vain,
Importunate wild cravings, that caress,
With pining lips its perfect emptiness!

IV.

Full in the fresh delight of victory,
    Young warriors! In your bridal garments drest,
On your death biers young virgin brides go by!
    Perish, young infants, on your mother's breast!
And you in love's first kiss, young lovers die,
    Dreaming of beauty still to be possest!
Let earth, thro' you, whose bliss no memory mars,
Send up one happy message to the stars!

V.

Say to them, you, " O wistful stars, down there,
    Hid in the depths of night's primeval dome
From your bright eyes, that seek her everywhere,
    Happiness dwells. From her abode we come.
There have we seen and known her; and we bear
    This message of the earth, her human home,
From star to star, through all your shining mists
Of suns and planets, ' Happiness exists '! "

VI.

Why do the stars with such reproachful eyes
    Search all the dismal avenues of night?
What questions that admit of no replies
    Come trembling to us on their plaintive light

" Alas ! " they seem to say, " earth's look belies
　　The tidings carried in their heavenward flight,
By these young messengers she sent us.　Yes,
They sung to us of earthly happiness."

VII.

" What have you done with it ?　Where is it ?　Who
　　Are its possessors ?　Yonder man, that glides
Down the dark alley stealthily, below
　　His cloak gleams something that he grasps and hides,
But can it be his happiness ?　Ah, no !
　　Hark ! through the sleeping house what harsh sound
　　　　grides,
I' the shuttered dark ?　　Doth happiness emit
That sullen cry ? or is it the centre-bit ?

VIII.

Is it for happiness dark hands explore
　　Those rummaged coffers ?　Is it happiness
You woman, hovering by the half-shut door,
　　On every passing stranger strives to press ?
Who are earth's happy ones ? and where their store
　　Of undiscoverable earthly bliss ?
Lurks it beneath the lids of eyes that keep
Its stolen treasures only while they sleep ? "

IX.

What to such questioners can we reply ?
　　Is all earth's happiness a heartless boast ?
Is it not lest the legend of earth's joy
　　Should all too soon become a legend lost,

That in their unsuspecting youth they die
  Who still believe in it?   And we (sad host
Of mourners !) hide our griefs, and whisper low,
Lest them, and it, our voice should disavow.

X.

For who would blast what those young lips have
    blest?
  Or who the promise they proclaimed, belie?
For their sakes, Sorrow, in thine aching breast
  Stifle the vain, involuntary sigh!
For their sakes, Misery, be thy groans suppressed !
  And smile, Old Age!   Lo, as thou limpest by,
Along the hedge, the honeysuckle flings,
Her frolic blossom and the linnet sings!

HUMAN DESTINIES.

SOME childhoods are there, that impatient pass
  Into life's sewer of common cares, almost
As rapid as the rinsings of a glass
  Down from the garret to the gutter tost
By some wild Magdalen, whose midnight mass
  Is a libation to the unlaid ghost
Of her slain innocence.   Where such drops fall
No blossoms spring.   The gutter takes them all.

Others there be, whose days are drops of dew
  That softly, droplet after droplet, sliding

From flower to flower, in sheltered peace pursue
  Hushed grassy courses; all their sweetness hiding,
Till from its silent growth a rivulet new
  The woodland wins, along whose wavelets gliding
On sunbeams and on moonbeams, fearless elves
Under dim forest leaves, disport themselves.

And there's a beauty that demands the light,
  Bursting like glory from the battle plain,
Full-blown.   A whole world's homage is its right;
  The sun is not solicited in vain;
He shines to be admired; from alpine height
  To height, from shore to shore, from main to main,
The god goes radiant, gilding, as it rolls,
Each wave between the Indus and the Poles.

But ah ! that beauty born beneath the veil,
  The Isis of the heart !   By many a fold
Its mystic vesture tells the silent tale
  Of charms that eyes profane may not behold.
Whilst to its own appointed priest the pale
  Composure of the sacred image, stoled
In sweet repose, if ruffled not, reveals
The secret it from all beside conceals.

Lift not the veil !   Divined in silence, leave
  The beauty hid beneath its holy hem !
Poësy, Childhood, Faith, Love, Passion, weave
  (Like the wise moth, ere round the rose's stem

With wavering joy his budded winglets heave)
  O'er them a mystery that shelters them
From the rude touch and the inquisitive eye.
Lift not the veil ; but worship and pass by !

THE FAMILY BOARD.

If in thy jaded spirit thou wouldst feel
  One hour of pure repose, and with repose
A careless joy !—go, join some family meal !
  How calm and full of cheerfulness life grows
Where, round one board, the commonplace appeal
  Of daily habit hath assembled those
Who dwell within its kind, familiar fold,
In unison together, young and old !

What sparkling expectation fills with light,
  The children's eyes !   How softly, one by one
From each parental forehead, out of sight,
  Fade the smoothed puckers, as the meal goes on.
How sociality aids appetite
  To improve the charm which it bestows upon
Plain wholesome dishes that are not " too good
And bright for human nature's daily food."

· · · · · · · ·

The children's rippling prattle that promotes
  The parents' grave, unruffled gaiety,
Like rivulets revelling along flowery moats
  Into calm rivers, they enrich thereby

Chance questions, light replies; gay anecdotes,
  Laughter, not loud but full of innocent joy,
The gurgling bottle and the chinking glass,
And little jokes that jostle as they pass!

The multifarious mirthfulness of these
  Interfluent sounds continued hovering
Around that table, like the restless bees
  That haunt the honied banquets of the Spring,
And in exchange for sweets and essences,
  Music and merriment to the blossoms bring,
As coming, going, humming, glowing they,
From flower to flower inquisitively stray.

From "*AFTER PARADISE; OR,
LEGENDS OF EXILE.*"

————

NORTH AND SOUTH.

I.

FAR in the southern night she sleeps;
   And there the heavens are husht, and there,
Low murmuring from the moonlit deeps,
   Faint music lulls the dreamful air.
No tears on her soft lashes hang,
   On her calm lips no kisses glow.
The throb, the passion, and the pang
       Are over now.

II.

But I?   From this full-peopled north,
   Whose midnight roar around me stirs,
How wildly still my heart goes forth
   To haunt that silent home of hers!

There night by night, with no release,
These sleepless eyes the vision see,
And all its visionary peace
But maddens me.

ATHENS.

THE burnt-out heart of Hellas here behold!
Quench'd fire-pit of the quick explosive Past,
Thought's highest crater—all its fervours cold,
Ashes and dust at last!

And what Hellenic light is living now
To gild, not Greece, but other lands, is given:
Not where the splendour sank, the after-glow
Of sunset stays in heaven.

But loud o'er Grecian ruins still the lark
Doth, as of old, Hyperion's glory hail,
And from Hymettus, in the moonlight, hark
The exuberant nightingale!

CINTRA.

I.

IN the brake are creaking
The tufted canes,
And the wind is streaking
With fugitive stains
A welkin haunted by hovering rains.

II.

Low lemon-boughs under
  My garden wall,
In the Quinta yonder,
  By fits let fall
Here an emerald leaf, there a pale gold ball,

III.

On the black earth, studded
  With droplets bright
From the fruit trees, budded,
  Some pink, some white,
And now overflooded with watery light.

IV.

For the sun, thro' a chasm
  Of the colourless air,
With a jubilant spasm
  From his broken lair
Upleaps and stands, for a moment, bare!

V.

But a breath bewilders
  The wavering weather;
And those sky-builders
  That put together
The vaporous walls of the cloud-bound ether

·VI.

From the mountains hasten
In pale displeasure
To mortice and fasten
The bright embrazure,
Shutting behind it day's innermost azure.

VII.

On the bleak blue rim
Of the lonesome lea,
Shapeless and dim
As far things at sea,
Mafra yon nebulous clump must be!

VIII.

Across the red furrows
To where in the sides
Of the hills he burrows
(As a reptile hides)
The many-legg'd, long-back'd, aqueduct strides

IX.

Just over the pines,
As from tapers snuff'd,
A thin smoke twines
Till its course is luff'd
At the edge of the cliff, by the breeze rebuff'd.

X.

Whence, downward turning
A dubious haze,
(From the charcoal burning)
It strays, delays,
And departs by a dozen different ways.

XI.

The chestnuts shiver,
The olive trees
Recoil and quiver,
Stung by the breeze,
Like sleepers awaked by a swarm of bees.

XII.

Down glimmering lanes
The grey oxen go;
And the grumbling wains
They drag onward slow
Wail, as they wind in a woeful row,

XIII.

With fruits and casks
To the seaside land,
Where Colares basks
In a glory bland,
And from gardens o'erhanging the scented sand

XIV.

Great aloes glisten
  And roses dangle.
But listen ! listen !
  The mule-bells jangle,
Rounding the rock-hewn path's sharp angle.

XV.

As their chime dies out
  The dim woods among,
With the ghostly shout
  And the distant song
Of the muleteers that have pass'd along,

XVI.

From behind the hill
  Whence comes that roar,
Up the road so still
  But a minute before ?
'Tis a message arrived from the grieved sea-
shore.

XVII.

And, tho' close it seems,
  Yet from far away
It is come, as in dreams
  The announcements they
To the souls that can understand convey.

XVIII.

For whenever you hear,
　　As you hear it now,
That sound so clear,
　　You may surely know
Foul weather's at hand, tho' no wind should
　　blow.

XIX.

But the cork wood is sighing,
　　It cannot find rest;
And the raven, flying
　　Around his black nest,
Hath signall'd the storm to the Sierra's crest.

XX.

Plaintive and sullen,
　　Penalva moans;
The torrents are swollen;
　　The granite bones
Of Cruzalta crackle with split pine cones;

XXI.

Roused and uproarious
　　The huge oaks yell
Till the ghost of Honorious
　　Is scared from his cell,
Where not even a ghost could in quietude dwell;

XXII.

For the woods all round
　　Its cork-clad walls
Are storm'd by the sound
　　Of the waterfalls
That have shatter'd their mountain pedestals.

XXIII.

On the topmost shelf
　　Of the Pena, fast
As the rock itself,
　　In a cluster vast
Stood castle and keep but a moment past;

XXIV.

Now, in what to the sight
　　Is but empty air,
They are vanisht quite,
　　And the sharp peak, bare
As a shaven chin, is upslanted there.

XXV.

Can a film of cloud,
　　Like the fiat of Fate,
In its sightless shroud
　　Thus obliterate
The ponderous mass of a pile so great?

XXVI.

'Twas a fact, yet a breath
    Has that fact dispell'd.
So truth, underneath
    A cloud compell'd
To hide her head, is no more beheld.

XXVII.

The achievement of years,
    By a minute effaced,
Departs, disappears,
    And is all replaced
By a cold blank colourless empty waste.

XXVIII.

All forms, alas,
    That remain or flee
As the winds that pass
    May their choice decree,
Stand faster far than have stood by me.

XXIX.

The man I served,
    And the woman I loved.
But what if they swerved
    As their faith was proved,
When a mountain can be by a mist removed?

SORRENTO REVISITED.

(1885.)

I.

On the lizarded wall and the gold-orb'd tree .
  Spring's splendour again is shining;
But the glow of its gladness awakes in me
  Only a vast repining.

II.

To Sorrento, asleep on the soft blue breast
  Of the sea that she loves, and dreaming,
Lone Capri uplifts an ethereal crest
  In the luminous azure gleaming.

III.

And the Sirens are singing again from the shore.
  'Tis the song that they sang to Ulysses;
But the sound of a song that is sung no more
  My soul in their music misses.

A SIGH.

The passion and the pain of yore
  Slow time hath still'd in vain,
Since all that I can feel no more
  I yearn to feel again.

NECROMANCY.

WHY didst thou let me deem thee lost for years,
  Youth of my heart? And, now that I have shed
O'er thy false grave long-since-forgotten tears,
  And put away my mourning for the dead,
And learn'd to live without thee half content,
  What brings thee back alive, tho' in disguise?
For thou, with this fair stranger's beauty blent,
  Art smiling on me thro' another's eyes.

STRANGERS.

(A RHAPSODY.)

CHILDREN are born, about whose lucid brows
The blue veins, visibly meandering, stream
Transparent : children in whose wistful eyes
Are looks like lost dumb creatures in a crowd,
That roam, and search, and find not what they seek.
These children are life's aliens.   The wise nurse
Shakes her head, murmuring, " They will not live !"
A piteous prophecy, yet best for them
The death that, pitifully premature,
Remits the pitiless penalty of birth ;
Letting the lost ones steal away unhurt,
Because unnoticed, from a world not theirs.

Strangers and star-born strayaways forlorn,
Who come so careless of the outlandish wealth
You carry with you, dropping as you go
Treasures beyond the reach of Orient Kings,

What seek you here where your unvalued gifts
Shall leave you beggars for an alms denied ?
Earth yields not their equivalent.   No field
So profitless but some poor price it hath ;
A spurious picture or a spavin'd horse
May find in time their willing purchasers ;
But never for its worth shall you exchange
A soul's unmarketable opulence.
And when at last, of those who (unenrich'd
By your impov'rishment) the gift forget,
Your thirst and hunger crave a broken crust,
A drop of water from the wayside well,
Stripes shall correct such importunities.

Linger not ! live not ! give not !   Hide your gifts,
Ungiven, deeper than Remembrance digs
Among the haunted ruins she explores
For riches lost.   And if abrupt mischance
Their buried store reveal, without a blush
Disown it, for a lie may sometimes save
A miser's life.   The truth would serve as well,
Were truth not unbelievable ; for, stored
In coin not current here and gems unprized,
Your treasures are worth nothing to the wretch
They tempt to make them, by a murder, his.
But this the assassins know not, and ill-arm'd,
Ill-arm'd and worse than weaponless, are you !
To whose inefficacious grasp was given
In solemn mockery the seraphic sword
That only archangelic hands can hold.
Your own have clutch'd it by the burning blade,
And, when you wield it, 'tis yourselves you wound.

You that have FEELING, think you to have all ?
Poor fools, and you have absolutely nought !

In reckonings of this world's arithmetic
Everything else is something by itself,
FEELING alone is nothing.   Could you add
That nothing to what counts for anything,
Forthwith a tenfold potency perchance
The unreckonable zero might bestow
Upon the reckon'd unit.   But what boots
A value so vicarious?
      Yours the spell
Whose all transfigurating sorceries
Convert the dust man grovels into gold ;
Robing the pauper royal in the pomp
Of princely exultations, changing night
To morning, death to life, the wilderness
To paradise ; beautifying pain,
Cleansing impurity, and strewing thick
The gulphs of Hell with starry gleams of Heaven.
But use it not !   Unsanction'd miracles
Are sentenced sins.   Writ large for all to read,
About the world's street corners Reason posts
"BEWARE OF THE MIRACULOUS !"   Whereto
Prudence appends, the placard to complete,
"MIRACLES ARE FORBIDDEN !"   Use it not,
Your gift unblest !   Lo, Virtue's High Priest comes,
Calls the Sanhedrim's long-phylacteried train,
Consults the scriptured scrolls, within them finds
No warrant for the wonders you perform,
And them and you doth anathematise.

Linger not ! live not ! give not !   All your gifts
Shall turn to stones and scourges in the hands
That crave them, and to live is to be lost.

 . . . .

Thou starry snowflake, whose still flight transforms
The frozen crystal's constellated crown

To an ethereal feather, seek not here,
Celestial strangers, seek not here on earth,
Where Purity were nameless but for thee,
The warmth that wastes, the fervours that defile !
Upon our wither'd branches hang not thou
Thy votive wreaths, nor our bleak paths invest
With thy pale presence ! Vainly dost thou cling
About our fasten'd casements, vainly spread
So close beside our doors thy spotless couch.
Behind them dwells Ingratitude. The voice
That welcomed thine arrival will anon
Resent thy lingering, and exclaim " Enough ! "
Trust not the looks that smile, the lips that sigh,
" I love thee ! " For to-day those words mean
      " Come ! "
To-morrow " Go ! " Men's words are numberless,
And yet in man's speech only the same word
Means " No " to-morrow that meant " Yes " to-day.

Linger not, live not, give not, you forlorn
Gift-laden strangers ! With your gifts ungiven,
And so at least undesecrated, die !

      .   .   .   .   .   .

What fills with such invincibility
The frail seed striving thro' the stubborn soil?
The sun so long one herbless spot caress'd,
That in the darkling germ beneath it stirr'd
A tender trouble, and that trouble seem'd
A promise. " Can it be, the Sun himself
Hath sought me ? He so glorious, he so great,
And I so dark, so insignificant !
Dear Sun, with all the strength thy love reveal'd,
Responding to thy summons, I am here ! "

And the rich life of granaried Lybia glows
Revelling already in a single grain.

Doth the Sun answer, 'Little one, too much
Thou hast responded, now respond no more?'
No, for throughout the illimitable heights
And deeps of boundless Being, to attain
It scarce suffices, at the most and best,
To tend beyond the unattainable,
And too much love is still not love enough.
The Sun may set, but all his rising wrought
To life's enraptured consciousness remains.
The Sun disowns not, even when he deserts,
What he put forth his fervours to evoke.
Man's love alone its doing disavows,
And makes denial of its dearest deed.

.   .   .   .
.

Beneath a dead bird's long-uncared-for cage,
That hangs forgotten in the cloister'd court
Of some lone uninhabitable house,
From the chink'd pavement slowly creeping comes
A thin weak stem that opens like a heart,
And puts forth tenderly two tiny hands
Of benediction to that cage forlorn,
Then dies, as tho' its little life had done
All it was born to do.   The flint-set earth
Requites the dead bird's gift—one casual seed,
And from her stony breast a blossom blows.

But, pouring forth Uranian star-seed, strew
Incipient heavens thro' all the hollowness
Of human gratitude for gifts divine,

And nothing from the sowing of such seed
Shall blossom but the bitterness of death.

.　　　.　　　.　　　.　　　.　　　.

O that the throbbing orb of this throng'd world,
The sun-led seasons, the revolving years,
Day with his glory, night with all her stars,
The present, and the future, and the past,
And earth, and heaven, should but a bauble be!
The unvalued gift of an extravagant soul,
Given undemanded, broken by a breath,
The sport of one exorbitant desire,
The easy spoil of one minute mischance,
And all for nothing!　What? the unheedful flint
Spares room to house the blossom that requites
A chance seed fallen from a dead bird's cage,
And nothing, nothing, in the long-long years,
That bring to other losses soon or late
The loss of loss remember'd, shall arise?
Nothing, not even a penitential tear,
A fleeting sigh, a momentary smile,
The benediction of a passing thought
Of pitiful remembrance—to repay
The quite-forgotten gift of too-much love!

.　　　.　　　.　　　.　　　.　　　.

All other loss comparison avails
To lessen, and all other ills worse ill
May mitigate.　Defeated monarchs find
Cold comfort left in Cæsar's legions lost:
The ruin'd merchant in the bankrupt state:
The bedless beggar in the bed-rid lord.
The sight of Niobe dries many tears,
And by the side of open graves are graves
Long seal'd, like old wounds cicatrised by time.

But this is an immitigable ill,
A lastingly incomparable loss,
A forfeiture of refuge that exiles
Its victim even from the lonest lodge
Where Misery's leprous outcasts may at least
Commiserate each other.   The excess
Of one o'erweening moment hath usurpt
The whole dominion of eternity;
Yet even the usurpation was a fraud,
For what seem'd all was nothing; and its dupes,
Who mourn that moment's loss, have with it lost
The right to say that it was ever theirs.

  . . .   . .

Sceptic, approach and, into this abysm
Of torment gazing, tremblingly believe!
Behold in Hell the soul's appalling proof
Of her dread immortality! What else
Could for a moment undestroy'd endure
The least of such annihilating pangs?
Transmute them into corporal sufferings.   Hurl
Their victim from the visionary top
Of some sky'd tower, and on its flinted base
Shatter his crumpled carcass: if the heart
Still beats, lay bare each lacerated nerve
And sear with scorching steel the sensitive flesh:
Or lift the bleeding ruins of the wretch,
Lay them in down, bandage with cruel care
The broken limbs, and nurse to life again
Their swooning anguish: then from eyes that burn
Chase slumber, and to lips that parch deny
Release from thirst.   It boots not!   Flesh and blood
Death to his painless sanctuary takes,
And life's material mechanism stops.
The first pang is the last.   But all these pangs

(And add to these what worse, if worse there be,
The torturer's teeming art hath yet devised)
Attain not the tenth part of those endured
Without cessation by the soul that loves,
When love is only suffering.   What escape,
What refuge, from self-torment hath the soul?
Or what for love is left unoverthrown
By love's own overthrow?

       The growth of love,
Outgrowing the wide girdle of the world,
Hath in itself absorb'd sun, moon, and stars,
Life, Death, and Thought's illimitable realm,
Leaving in Time no moment, and in Space
No point, its omnipresence kindles not
To palpitant incandescence—and what then?
A word, nay not so much, a breath unbreathed,
A look, and all this universe of love,
Cramm'd with the curse of Tantalus, becomes
A pitiless infinitude of fierce
Importunate impossibilities,
Where nothing is but what may never be.

. . . .

Fond wretch, with those insatiable eyes,
Among the ruins of a world destroy'd
What art thou seeking?   Its destroyer?   Look!
He stands before thee.   And thou know'st him not.
The traitor of thy perisht universe
Hath perisht with it.   Nay, that world and he,
Whose creature and creator was thyself,
Save in thyself existed not.   Away,
Disown'd survivor of what never was!

. . . .

There is a sigh that hath no audible sound,

And, like a ghost that hath no visible form,
Breathing unheard thro' solitudes unseen,
Its presence haunts the Desert of the Heart.
Fata Morgana! Fair Enchantress, Queen
Of all that ever-quivering quietness,
There dost thou dreaming dwell, and there create
Those fervid desolations of delight,
Where dwell with thee the joys that never were!

And, when in darkness fades the phantom scene,
The wizard stars that nightly trembling light
That undiscover'd loneliness are looks
From eyes that love no longer.   All the winds
That whisper there are breaths of broken vows
And perjured promises.   The pale mirage
That haunts the simmering hyaline above
Is all the work of ghosts, and its bright wastes
Teem with fantastic spectres of the swoons
Of prostrate passions, hopes become despairs,
And dreams of bliss unblest.   In that weird sky
There is no peace, but a perpetual trance
Of torturous ecstasy.   Vext multitudes
Of frantic apparitions mingle there,
And part, and vanish, waving vaporous arms
Of supplication—to each other lured,
And by each other pantingly repulsed.
The goblin picture of a passionate world
Painted on nothingness !   And all the sands,
Heaved by the sultry sighings of the heart
Of this unquietable solitude,
Are waves that everlastingly roll on
O'er wrecks deep-sunken in a shoreless sea
Whose bed is vast oblivion.   Out of sight,
Into that sea's abysmal bosom pour'd,
Flow all desires unsatisfied, all pains

Unpitied, all affections unfulfill'd.
And sighs, and tears, and smiles misunderstood.

There all the adventurous argosies that sail'd
In search of undiscover'd worlds, reduced
To undiscoverable wrecks, remain.
And there perchance, at last, no more estranged
From all around them, since not strangers they
Than all things else, where all things else are
    strange,
In that wide strangeness unrejected rest
The world's rejected strangers——loves unloved,
And lives unlived, and longings unappeased.

—————

URIEL.

(A MYSTERY.)

—————

DEDICATION.

To you, the dead and gone, bright-eyed Desires
Whose beauty lights no more my dwindled day,
Here, sitting lone beside forsaken fires,
    I dedicate this lay.

I.

I HEARD a Voice by night, that called to me
    "Uriel! Uriel!"
The night was dark, and nothing could I see,
Yet knew I by the voice that it was She

Whom my soul loves so well
That when She calls Her follower I must be,
Whether She call from Heaven or from Hell.

II.

Then to the Voice, " What is thy will ? " said I.
But for sole response thro' the darkness fell,
Repeated with the same importunate cry,
Mine own name only, " Uriel! Uriel! "
I could not sleep nor rest upon my bed,
So I rose up, and thro' the husht house pass'd
With steps unlighted (for my lamp was dead)
Out on the heath.

III.

That Voice flew onward fast,
Still calling, and still onward after it
I followed, far outsped: for there, beneath
The moonless heaven, not even a marsh-fire lit
Night's fearful sameness; and athwart the heath,
Not fast and free as flew the Voice that led,
But halting oft, my steps went stumblingly.
Each footstep, as it fell, recoil'd with dread
From what it toucht; and, tho' I could not see,
I felt that, where I trod, the plain was spread
With corpses.   Heap'd so thick they seem'd to be
That I, at every moment, fear'd to tread
Upon a dead man's face.   Yet, undeterr'd,
My feet obey'd a will not mine, whose spell
Their course constrain'd.   For still that Voice I
      heard,
And still the Voice called " Uriel! Uriel! "

At last a livid light began to grow
Low down in heaven.   It was the moon that, pent
Behind a slowly crumbling cloud till now,
Athwart thin flakes of worn-out vapour sent
A filmy gleam.   And I could see thereby
The corpses that lay litter'd on the heath.
Each white up-slanted face and unshut eye
Was staring at me with the stare of death:
Harnessed in rusty mail from head to heel
Was each dead body: and each dead right hand
Grasp'd by the hilt a blade of bloodstained steel,
But broken was each blade.   And, while I scann'd
Those dead men's faces, I began to feel
A sadness which I could not understand:
But unto me it seem'd that I had seen,
And known, and loved them, somewhere, long ago:
Tho' when, or where, and all that was between
That time and this (if what perplexed me so
With mimic memories had indeed once been)
I knew no longer.   On this fatal plain
Vast battle must have once been waged, so keen
That none was spared by the relentless foe
For unmolested burial of the slain.

v.

And, as I gazed upon them, wondering why
These unrememberable faces seem'd
Mysteriously familiar to mine eye,
The cloudy light that on their corselets gleam'd
Grew clearer, and a sound began to swell
Moaning along the heath: the swarthy sky

Was scourged by a strong wind: the moonlight
    stream'd,
Flooding the land: and on the dead men fell
Its frigid splendour.   Then stark upright rose
Each dead man, shouting " Uriel! Uriel!"
And in the windy air aloft all those
Arm'd corpses waved their shatter'd swords.

VI.

                  I cried,
" What are ye? and what name is it you bear?
Corpses or ghosts?   Is Life with Death allied,
To breed new horrors in this hideous lair
Of Desolation?"   And they all replied
" Thine is our name, for thine our Legions were,
And thine would still be, if thou hadst not died.
But corpse or ghost thou art thyself, and how
Should we thy death survive?   It is not well
When the dead do not know the dead, nor know
The date of their own death-day, Uriel!
Our leader bold in many a fight wast thou,
And we fought bravely.   But thy foes and ours
Were strongest.   And the strife is over now,
And we be all dead men.   And those tall towers
We built are fallen, all our banners torn,
All our swords broken, all our strong watch fires
Quencht, and in death have we been left forlorn
Of sepulture, tho' sons of princely sires,
Born to find burial fair with saints and kings,
Where, over trophied tombs, the taper shines
On tablets rich with votive offerings,
And priestly perfumes soothe memorial shrines.
And that is why we cannot find repose
In the bare quiet of unburied death;

But ever, when at night the wild wind blows
Upon the barren bosom of this heath,
Our dead flesh tingles, and revives, and glows
With the brief passion of a borrow'd breath,
Breathed by the wind: and on as the wind goes
Go with the wind we must, where'er that be,
A lonesome pilgrimage along the night,
Till the wind falls again, and with it we.
Farewell!"

VII.

The wild wind swept them from my sight,
Even as they spake, and all the heath was bare.
Sighingly the wind ceased.   The night was still.
The dead were gone.   Only the moonlight there
Upon the empty heath lay clear and chill
Then I remember'd long-forgotten things,
And all my loss.   I could not farther fare
Along that haunted heath; for my heart's strings
Were aching, gnaw'd by an immense despair.
Flat on the spot where last they stood I fell,
And clutch'd the wither'd fern, as one that clings
Fast to a grave where all he loved lies dead,
And wept, and wept, and wept.
                                        "Rise, Uriel,"
The Voice I knew still call'd, "and follow me!"
But I could only weep, so vast a well
Of tears within me flow'd.   At last I said
"What heart or hope have I to follow thee?
Are not the Legions lost, that at thy call
To mine own overthrow and theirs I led?
For I have seen again their faces all,
And death was all I saw there."   "Let them be!"
The Voice replied, "The dead shall live again
When we have reach'd the goal whereto I go,

And there shalt thou rejoin them.   Nor till then
Can'st thou thyself return to life, for thou
Thyself art also fall'n among the slain.
But look upon me, faithless one, and know
That I am life in death, and joy in pain,
And light in darkness."

VIII.

                    I look'd up, and saw,
In glory that was not of mere moonlight,
(Glory that filled me with a great glad awe)
Shining above me, Her my soul loves well,
Like a white Angel.   And along the night
Her voice still call'd me, "Uriel! Uriel!"
Again I follow'd.   And it seem'd that days,
And nights, and weeks, and months, and years went
    by,
And on we went by never-ending ways,
Thro' worlds and worlds.   And ever was mine
    eye
Fixt on that beckoning Form with faithful gaze.
And seasons little cared for—shine or shade,
Or heat or cold—pursued us.   Many a Spring,
And many a Summer, many an Autumn, stay'd
My panting path, and round me strove to fling
Their fervid arms, and many a Winter made
His frozen fingers meet and fiercely cling
In lean embrace that long my course delay'd,
And Pain and Pleasure both essay'd to wring
My purpose from me.   But still, sore afraid
Lest I should lose my Guide by tarrying,
Forward I press'd whenever the Voice said
"Uriel! Uriel! linger not."

IX.

At last
We reach'd what seem'd the end of a dead world.
Wall'd round it was by mountains bare and vast,
And thro' them one thin perilous pathway curl'd
Into an unknown land of ice and snow,
Where nothing lived, nor aught was left to freeze
But frost.   There was a heap of bones below;
Above, a flock of vultures.   Under these,
Hard by a stream that long had ceased to flow,
A miserable, squalid, lean old man,
Nursing a broken harp upon his knees,
Sat in the frozen pass.   His eyes were wan,
But full of spiteful looks.   She my soul loved,
Fair as a skyward Seraph on the wing,
Before me up that perilous pathway moved,
Calling me from above, and beckoning.
But he that sat before the pass began
To twang his harp, which had but one shrill string,
(Whose notes like icy needles thro' me ran
And with a crack'd and creaking voice to sing
"O fool, infatuated fool, forbear!
For yonder is the Land of Ice and Snow,
And She is dead that beckoneth to thee there,
And dead forever are the dead, I know."

Whilst thus that lean old man, with eyes aglare,
Sang to his broken harp's one string below,
The vultures scream'd above in the bleak air
"Dead are the dead forever!"

X.

"What art thou,
Malignant wretch?" I cried.   The old man said

" I am the Ancient Porter of this Pass,
Beyond which lies the Land of Ice and Snow.
And all the dwellers in that land are dead,
And dead forever are the dead, I know.
And this, my harp—I know not when, alas !
But all its strings were broken long ago,
Save one, which time makes tough.   The others
     were
Of sweeter tone, but this sounds more intense.
And, for my name, some say it is Despair,
And others say it is Experience."

Thereat he laugh'd, and shook his sordid rags,
And his wan eyes with sullen malice gleam'd.
And loud again, upon the icy crags,
In that bleak air above, the vultures scream'd.

TRANSFORMATIONS.

(A MIDSUMMER NIGHT'S DREAM).

I.

" HERE at last alone,
You and I together!
All the night our own,
And the warm June weather!
Not a soul in sight!
What we will, we may.
Nothing is by night
As it was by day.
Look around you!   See,

All things change themselves.
Blossom, bower and tree
Turn to Fays and Elves:
Trivial things and common
Into rare things rising.
Why should man and woman
Be less enterprising?
Fashion's formal creatures
We till now have been,
With prim-patterned features
And a borrow'd mien,
Now the mask is broken,
Now the fetters fall,
Wishes long unspoken
Now are all in all!
Wondrous transformation
Now, for you and me,
Waits our invocation.
Say, what shall we be?"

II.

"What you will," said She.

III.

"Look, then, and listen! For you must be
   waiting,
Behind a high grating,
The sound of my signal. Along the wild land
I have gallop'd full speed on my coal-black
   steed
To free my love from my foeman's hand.
And lo! in the moonlight alert I stand
Close under the castle wall.

Look out, I am here!
Leap down, nor fear!
For into my rescuing arms you fall,
Safe and free.   They are round you, see!
One saddle must serve us, so cling to me well,
And away, and away, thro' the night we flee!
But hark!   'Tis the clang of the 'larum bell.
Our pursuers awake.   For dear life's sake
Cling to me closer and closer still,
And speed, speed, my coal-black steed!
They are hurrying after us over the hill,
But clear'd is the river, and cross'd is the heath,
Deep into the sheltering woods we dart,
And O what a ride! for I feel your breath,
And how hot it burns! and I hear your heart,
And how loud it beats! as I laugh ' We part
No more, come life, come death!'"

IV.

" No, no,"
She sighed, "not so!
Too fiercely fleets your coal-black steed,
And pleasure faints in passion's speed,
And the bliss that lingers the best must be."
Sighed She.   .

V.

"Listen, then, and look, once more!
We are sailing round a southern island.
Fragrant breathes the dusky shore,
Folded under many a moonlit highland.
Fragrant breathes the dusky shore,

And where dips the languid oar
Wavelets dimple, flash and darkle,
Odours wander, fireflies sparkle:
Thro' them all our bark is gliding,
Gliding softly, gliding slowly:
Not a cloud their sweetness hiding,
And the heavens are husht and holy:
Midnight's panting pulse uncertain
Faintly fans the heaving curtain
O'er the silken-pillow'd seat
Where you lie with slippered feet,
Tresses loosed and zone unbound;
While, my ribbon'd lute unslinging,
I, your troubadour, beside you,
O'er its chords, that trembling sound,
Pour the song my soul is singing:
List, and let its music guide you,
Till the goal of dreams is found!"

VI.

"Ah, stay so!"
She murmured low,
"Song and stream forever flow!
And if this be dreaming, never
Let me wake, but dream for ever,
Dreaming thus, if dream it be!"
Then He:

VII.

"As night's magic blends together
Moonbeams, starbeams, odours, dews,
In a hush of happy weather,

Earth and heaven to interfuse;
So my song draws softly down
All your soul into my own,
Bounteous gift on gift bestowing:
First that heaven, your face; and then
Heaven's divinest stars, those eyes
Under dewy lashes glowing;
Last, those lips, whose smile caresses
All their breath beatifies;
And the fragrance o'er me flowing
From those downward shaken tresses,
Whose delicious wildernesses
Hide such haunts of happy sighs!"

VIII.

" Rise, ah rise!"
Faint She whispered. "Hold me fast!
Far away the fixt earth flies,
And I know not where we are.
What is coming? What is past?
Bursting, flashing, fleeting, see,
Swiftly star succeeds to star
Till . . . . in what new world we are?"
" Love's," said He.

IX.

"Song and lute the spell obeying,
Cease in silence, sweeter, stronger,
Than song-singing or lute-playing;
And, entranced, I know no longer

Whither are my senses straying:
But I feel my spirit blending
With the bliss of thine, and ending
Tremulously lost in thee!"

X.

"Hush!" sighed She,
Lest this dream, if dream alone
And no more than dream it be,
By a breath should be undone.
For "ah," She sighed,
"I and thou, what are we now?"
And He replied,
"Thou art I, and I am thou,
And we are one!"

—— — — — ——

THE WALTER SCOTT PRESS, NEWCASTLE-ON-TYNE

THE CANTERBURY POETS.

EDITED BY WILLIAM SHARP.

IN SHILLING VOLUMES, CLOTH, SQUARE 8VO.

Cloth, Red Edges · 1s.	*Red Roan, Gilt Edges,* 2s. 6d
Cloth, Uncut Edges · · 1s.	*Pad. Morocco, Gilt Edges* · 5s.

ALREADY ISSUED.

Christian Year.	Bowles, Lamb, etc.
Coleridge.	Early English Poetry.
Longfellow.	Sea Music.
Campbell.	Herrick.
Shelley.	Ballades and Rondeaus.
Wordsworth.	Irish Minstrelsy.
Blake.	Milton's Paradise Lost.
Whittier.	Jacobite Ballads.
Poe.	Australian Ballads.
Chatterton.	Moore's Poems.
Burns. Poems.	Border Ballads.
Burns. Songs.	Song-Tide.
Marlowe.	Odes of Horace.
Keats.	Ossian.
Herbert.	Elfin Music.
Victor Hugo.	Southey.
Cowper.	Chaucer.
Shakespeare:	Poems of Wild Life.
Songs, Poems, and Sonnets.	Paradise Regained.
Emerson.	Crabbe.
Sonnets of this Century.	Dora Greenwell.
Whitman.	Goethe's Faust.
Scott. Marmion, etc.	American Sonnets.
Scott. Lady of the Lake, etc.	Landor's Poems.
Praed.	Greek Anthology.
Hogg.	Hunt and Hood.
Goldsmith.	Humorous Poems.
Mackay's Love Letters.	Lytton's Plays.
Spenser.	Great Odes.
Children of the Poets.	Owen Meredith's Poems.
Ben Jonson.	Painter-Poets.
Byron (2 Vols.).	Women-Poets.
Sonnets of Europe.	Love Lyrics.
Allan Ramsay.	American Humor. Verse
Sydney Dobell.	Scottish Minor Poets.
Days of the Year.	Cavalier Lyrists.
Pope.	German Ballads.
Heine.	Songs of Beranger.
Beaumont and Fletcher.	Poems by Roden Noel.

London: WALTER SCOTT, LIMITED, 24 Warwick Lane.

SELECTED THREE VOLUME SETS

IN NEW BROCADE BINDING.

6s. per Set, in Shell Case to match.

Also Bound in Roan, in Shell Case, 9s. per Set.

O. W. HOLMES SERIES—

Autocrat of the Breakfast Table.

The Professor at the Breakfast Table.

The Poet at the Breakfast Table.

LANDOR SERIES—

Landor's Imaginary Conversations.

Pentameron.

Pericles and Aspasia.

THREE ENGLISH ESSAYISTS—

Essays of Elia.

Essays of Leigh Hunt.

Essays of William Hazlitt.

THREE CLASSICAL MORALISTS—

Meditations of Marcus Aurelius.

Teaching of Epictetus.

Morals of Seneca.

WALDEN SERIES—

Thoreau's Walden.

Thoreau's Week.

Thoreau's Essays.

FAMOUS LETTERS

Letters of Burns.

Letters of Byron.

Letters of Chesterfield

LOWELL SERIES—

My Study Windows.

The English Poets.

The Biglow Papers.

London : WALTER SCOTT, 24 Warwick Lane, Paternoster Row.

NEW TWO-VOLUME PROSE SETS.

IN NEW BROCADE BINDING,

4s. per Set, in Shell Case to match.

MALORY'S HISTORY OF KING ARTHUR.

MALORY'S MARVELLOUS ADVENTURES.

———

ENGLISH FAIRY TALES.

IRISH FAIRY TALES.

———

HEINE'S PROSE.

HEINE'S TRAVEL-SKETCHES.

———

WHITE'S SELBORNE.

MITFORD'S OUR VILLAGE

WHITMAN'S SPECIMEN DAYS.

WHITMAN'S DEMOCRATIC VISTAS.

———

GREAT PAINTERS.

GREAT COMPOSERS.

———

SENECA'S MORALS.

ANNALS OF TACITUS.

———

EMERSON'S ESSAYS.

SARTOR RESARTUS.

———

VICAR OF WAKEFIELD.

JANE EYRE.

London: WALTER SCOTT, LIMITED, 24 Warwick Lane.

THE SCOTT LIBRARY.

Cloth, uncut edges, gilt top.   Price 1/6 per volume.

ALREADY ISSUED.

THE SCOTT LIBRARY—continued.

English Prose.

The Pillars of Society.

Fairy and Folk Tales.

Essays of Dr. Johnson.

Essays of Wm. Hazlitt.

Landor's Pentameron, &c.

Poe's Tales and Essays

Vicar of Wakefield.

Political Orations.

Autocrat of the Breakfast-Table.

Poet at the Breakfast-Table.

Professor at the Breakfast-Table.

Chesterfield's Letters.

Stories from Carleton.

Jane Eyre.

Elizabethan England.

Davis's Writings.

Spence's Anecdotes

More's Utopia.

Sadi's Gulistan.

English Folk Tales.

Northern Studies.

Famous Reviews.

Aristotle's Ethics.

Landor's Aspasia.

Tacitus.

Essays of Elia.

Balzac.

De Musset's Comedies.

Darwin's Coral-Reefs.

Sheridan's Plays.

Our Village.

Humphrey's Clock, &c.

Tales from Wonderland

Douglas Jerrold.

Rights of Woman.

Athenian Oracle.

Essays of Sainte-Beuve.

Selections from Plato.

Heine's Travel Sketches.

Maid of Orleans.

Sydney Smith.

The New Spirit.

Marvellous Adventures.
(From the Morte d'Arthur.)

Helps's Essays.

London: WALTER SCOTT, LIMITED, 24 Warwick Lane.

New Series of Critical Biographies.

Edited by ERIC ROBERTSON and FRANK T. MARZIALS.

GREAT WRITERS.

Cloth, Gilt Top, Price 1s. 6d.

ALREADY ISSUED—

LIFE OF LONGFELLOW. By Prof. E. S. ROBERTSON.

LIFE OF COLERIDGE. By HALL CAINE.

LIFE OF DICKENS. By FRANK T. MARZIALS.

LIFE OF D. G. ROSSETTI. By JOSEPH KNIGHT.

LIFE OF SAMUEL JOHNSON. By Col. F. GRANT.

LIFE OF DARWIN. By G. T. BETTANY.

CHARLOTTE BRONTE. By AUGUSTINE BIRRELL.

LIFE OF CARLYLE. By RICHARD GARNETT, LL.D.

LIFE OF ADAM SMITH. By R. B. HALDANE, M.P.

LIFE OF KEATS. By W. M. ROSSETTI.

LIFE OF SHELLEY. By WILLIAM SHARP.

LIFE OF SMOLLETT. By DAVID HANNAY.

LIFE OF GOLDSMITH. By AUSTIN DOBSON.

LIFE OF SCOTT. By Professor YONGE.

LIFE OF BURNS. By Professor BLACKIE.

LIFE OF VICTOR HUGO. By FRANK T. MARZIALS.

LIFE OF EMERSON. By RICHARD GARNETT, LL.D.

LIFE OF GOETHE. By James Sime.

LIFE OF CONGREVE. By Edmund Gosse.

LIFE OF BUNYAN. By Canon Venables.

LIFE OF CRABBE. By T. E. Kebbel, M.A.

LIFE OF HEINE. By William Sharp.

LIFE OF MILL. By W. L. Courtney.

LIFE OF SCHILLER. By H. W. Nevinson.

LIFE OF CAPTAIN MARRYAT. By David Hannay.

LIFE OF LESSING. By T. W. Rolleston.

LIFE OF MILTON. By Richard Garnett.

LIFE OF GEORGE ELIOT. By Oscar Browning.

LIFE OF BALZAC. By Frederick Wedmore.

LIFE OF JANE AUSTEN. By Goldwin Smith.

LIFE OF BROWNING. By William Sharp.

LIFE OF BYRON. By Hon. Roden Noel.

LIFE OF HAWTHORNE. By Moncure Conway.

LIFE OF SCHOPENHAUER. By Professor Wallace.

LIFE OF SHERIDAN. By Lloyd Sanders.

LIFE OF THACKERAY. By Herman Merivale and Frank T. Marzials.

LIFE OF CERVANTES. By W. E. Watts.

LIFE OF VOLTAIRE. By Francis Espinasse.

Bibliography to each, by J. P. Anderson, British Museum.

LIBRARY EDITION OF "GREAT WRITERS."

Printed on large paper of extra quality, in handsome binding, Demy 8vo, price 2s. 6d. per volume.

London : Walter Scott, Limited, 24 Warwick Lane.

COMPACT AND PRACTICAL.

In Limp Cloth; for the Pocket. Price One Shilling.

THE EUROPEAN
CONVERSATION BOOKS.

FRENCH.   ITALIAN.
SPANISH.   GERMAN.
NORWEGIAN.

CONTENTS.

Hints to Travellers—Everyday Expressions—Arriving at and Leaving a Railway Station — Custom House Enquiries—In a Train—At a Buffet and Restaurant— At an Hotel—Paying an Hotel Bill—Enquiries in a Town—On Board Ship—Embarking and Disembarking —Excursion by Carriage—Enquiries as to Diligences— Enquiries as to Boats—Engaging Apartments—Washing List and Days of Week — Restaurant Vocabulary — Telegrams and Letters, etc., etc.

The contents of these little handbooks are so arranged as to permit direct and immediate reference. All dialogues or enquiries not considered absolutely essential have been purposely excluded, nothing being introduced which might confuse the traveller rather than assist him. A few hints are given in the introduction which will be found valuable to those unaccustomed to foreign travel.

London: WALTER SCOTT. LIMITED, 24 Warwick Lane.

Crown 8vo, Cloth.   Price 3s. 6d. per Vol.; Half Mor., 6s. 6d.

THE
CONTEMPORARY SCIENCE SERIES.

EDITED BY HAVELOCK ELLIS.

Illustrated Volumes containing between 300 and 400 pp.

THE CONTEMPORARY SCIENCE SERIES will bring within general reach of the English-speaking public the best that is known and thought in all departments of modern scientific research. The influence of the scientific spirit is now rapidly spreading in every field of human activity. Social progress, it is felt, must be guided and accompanied by accurate knowledge,—knowledge which is, in many departments, not yet open to the English reader. In the Contemporary Science Series all the questions of modern life—the various social and politico-economical problems of to-day, the most recent researches in the knowledge of man, the past and present experiences of the race, and the nature of its environment—will be frankly investigated and clearly presented.

First Volumes of the Series:—

EVOLUTION OF SEX. By Prof. GEDDES and THOMSON.
ELECTRICITY IN MODERN LIFE. G. W. DE TUNZELMANN.
THE ORIGIN OF THE ARYANS. By Dr. ISAAC TAYLOR.
PHYSIOGNOMY AND EXPRESSION. By P. MANTEGAZZA.
EVOLUTION AND DISEASE. By J. B. SUTTON.
THE VILLAGE COMMUNITY. By G. L. GOMME.
THE CRIMINAL. By HAVELOCK ELLIS.
SANITY AND INSANITY. By Dr. C. MERCIER.
HYPNOTISM. By Dr. ALBERT MOLL (Berlin).
MANUAL TRAINING. By Dr. WOODWARD (St. Louis, Mo.).
THE SCIENCE OF FAIRY TALES. By E. S. HARTLAND.
PRIMITIVE FOLK. By ELIE RECLUS.
THE EVOLUTION OF MARRIAGE. By LETOURNEAU.
BACTERIA AND THEIR PRODUCTS. By Dr. WOODHEAD.
EDUCATION AND HEREDITY. By J. M. GUYAU.
THE MAN OF GENIUS. By Prof. LOMBROSO.
THE GRAMMAR OF SCIENCE. By Prof. KARL PEARSON.
PROPERTY: ITS ORIGIN. By CH. LETOURNEAU.
VOLCANOES, PAST AND PRESENT. By Prof. E. HULL.
PUBLIC HEALTH PROBLEMS. By Dr. J. F. J. SYKES.

LONDON: WALTER SCOTT, LIMITED, 24 WARWICK LANE.

PEER GYNT: A Dramatic Poem.

BY HENRIK IBSEN.

Translated by WILLIAM AND CHARLES ARCHER.

This Translation, though unrhymed, preserves throughout the various rhythms of the original.

———

"To English readers this will not merely be a new work of the Norwegian poet, dramatist, and satirist, but it will also be a new Ibsen. . . . Here is the imaginative Ibsen, indeed, the Ibsen of such a boisterous, irresistible fertility of fancy that one breathes with difficulty as one follows him on his headlong course. . . '*Peer Gynt*' is a fantastical satirical drama of enormous interest, and the present translation of it is a masterpiece of fluent, powerful, graceful, and literal rendering."—*The Daily Chronicle.*

London : WALTER SCOTT, LIMITED, 24 Warwick Lane.

Foolscap 8vo, Cloth, Price 3s. 6d.

———

THE INSPECTOR-GENERAL

(Or "REVIZÓR.")

A RUSSIAN COMEDY.

By NIKOLAI VASILIYEVICH GOGOL.

Translated from the original Russian, with Introduction and Notes, by **A. A. SYKES**, B.A., Trinity College, Cambridge.

———

Though one of the most brilliant and characteristic of Gogol's works, and well known on the Continent, the present is the first translation of his *Revizór*, or Inspector-General, which has appeared in English. A satire on Russian administrative functionaries, the *Revizór* is a comedy marked by continuous gaiety and invention, full of "situation," each development of the story accentuating the satire and emphasising the characterisation, the whole play being instinct with life and interest. Every here and there occurs the note of caprice, of naïveté, of unexpected fancy, characteristically Russian. The present translation will be found to be admirably fluent, idiomatic, and effective.

London: WALTER SCOTT, LIMITED, 24 Warwick Lane.

IBSEN'S PROSE DRAMAS

EDITED BY WILLIAM ARCHER.

In Five Volumes.

Crown 8vo, Cloth, Price 3s. 6d. Per Volume.

VOL. I.

"A DOLL'S HOUSE," "THE LEAGUE OF YOUTH," and "THE PILLARS OF SOCIETY."

VOL. II.

"GHOSTS," "AN ENEMY OF THE PEOPLE," and "THE WILD DUCK."

VOL III.

"LADY INGER OF ÖSTRÅT," "THE VIKINGS AT HELGELAND," "THE PRETENDERS."

VOL IV.

'EMPEROR AND GALILEAN." With an Introductory Note by WILLIAM ARCHER.

VOL. V.

"ROSMERSHOLM"; "THE LADY FROM THE SEA"; "HEDDA GABLER." Translated by WILLIAM ARCHER.

London : WALTER SCOTT, 24 Warwick Lane, Paternoster Row.

www.ingramcontent.com/pod-product-compliance
Lightning Source LLC
Chambersburg PA
CBHW020901020726
47497CB00005B/1511